Twin Flames

Twin Flames

by

Rhonda Michelle Rankin Evans

Everlasting Publishing
Yakima, Washington
USA

Twin Flames
by
Rhonda Michelle Rankin Evans

ISBN: 978-0-9983858-9-1

First Edition
Everlasting Publishing
PO Box 1061
Yakima, Washington 98907
USA

Dedication

In memory of my dear late grandmother (Bigmama). It was she the late great Mary Glover Steele that taught me; my life is not for myself, but that God may be lifted to His Holy temple by my life. That the world would see his miraculous works through me. I am God's humble servant grandmother.

In dedication to my seven children; who were selfishly brought into this world by me in search and need of love. Thank you to my oldest three children Frank, Tezia, and Alex for enduring and loving me through my crazy teen years when being a mother was not how I operated during your early years. You have watched God's process turn me into the woman I am today, although it has been painful to see me do better with the youngest three. I thank God you are still here growing with me. To my youngest three, it has not been easy many parenting classes and anger management classes and therapy. It was all seven of you who gave me a reason to live. Now you're all grown I have learned many lessons to take to the world and beyond. You are all my super heroes. Now it's to infinity and beyond.

Love,

Mommy

"Twin Flames"

"The journey begins when we first start it in the Master's hands."

"Twin Flames"
The merging of two lifestyles

Introduction

Story 1. Moreo Conquers fear/PTSD

Story 2. Tackling Religious belief differences. (a simple honest conversation can do wonders)

Story 3. Merging blended families while dealing with major emotional insecurities. (don't be so easily offended this may be a healing moment for god to get glory in)

Story 4. Financial Stability, Moreo takes a big financial loss that rocks his ego. (Help meet means also helping to get things back on track financially)

Story 5. Dealing with ex's and the residual effects of previous relationships. (sometimes prayer may need a little assistance breaking the devils back. (joking but very serious)

Story 6. Dealing with death, Rena's mother passes and she is unaware of how it impacts her initially. (Moreo ministers into his wife healing words of strength)

Story 7. Moving back to the States, choosing a location suitable for the entire family. (Location can make or brake all that you've worked hard to build.)

Story 8. Sexual issues and intimacy age and high blood pressure forces Moreo to give up his ego, to pure love. (Moreo and Rena lived their lives for God and before the world as a holy righteous symbol of God's love and concern for humanity and all that concerns us including our love lives.

Twin Flames

Introduction

The story of Moreo and Rena all started many years ago in a small town in the state of North Carolina. We shall call this place Saltzburgh. Both were children who came from military backgrounds. Moreo's father was an Army soldier and Rena's father was a Navy Seaman, they both had very troubled mother's who may or may not have married such men, who were also troubled.

They both endured many forms of abuse early on in their youth beginning with mental and verbal as their fathers both began to heavily depend on alcohol as their sources of inspiration. They would get drunk and beat on the children's mothers and it got so violent Moreo and Rena both had to suffer their parents divorcing and the traumatic experiences that would follow that.

Moreo was left behind by his mother to live with his father, who still would suffer from alcoholism for much longer after divorcing Christine Moreo's mother. Young Mr. Ellroy would endure physical abuse verbal abuse and mental as well as sexual abuse. He was traumatized and yet went to school daily as if nothing was going on in his home. He was very strong willed with a good head on his shoulders. Thanks to his mom taking he and siblings to church when they were very young.

Rena was a year older than Moreo, but she had been held back and that's how they met. You see Rena still had to live with her mother where she was physically tormented and when she would visit her family members' houses she would be sexually assaulted by male and females. Her mom was a partying woman and Rena could end up with anybody as a babysitter. Rena also was sexually assaulted by her father who two weeks later committed suicide on Rena's mom's front porch. Thank God Rena was not there, no telling what might have happened to her or the effect of added trauma.

Moreo took the high road as far as not lashing out on society around him. Rena on the other hand, was very angry and hurt with God because she never forgot her promise to Him. She promised God that she would use her life as his tool on earth to love, heal, and lead his lost beloved children back to Him and right loving righteous knowledge of the Master.

So how could her life be so brutal? Her parents were not all the fails in Rena's life. At the ripe old age of fourteen she wanted her own love a baby. She decided that her boyfriend Fredrick would be a good father for her first child his was kind to her and very gentle, she thought. At age sixteen Rena gave birth to her oldest child Fredrick the third. As his dad was a Jr. She had now found someone she thought would love her no matter what until death. She had her very own child, as Rena understood it because she still loved her parents and forgave them, it was just her mom could not forgive herself and let Rena in. Rena's father was dead. Rena thanked God daily and honored him for the times she was with her grandmother. Her grandmother started getting Rena for long periods of time at age three. By the time Rena was four she was reading the bible and on the 4-H club. When she came back at age eight after being with her mom from five until, she learned from her grandmother how to fast with intent and pray fervently. She was taught how the spirit works and what scriptures are living words of powerful and absolute healing. She also learned how to cook her favorite foods at that time in her life. She was eleven is when the separation between Rena and her grandmother began. It was a very traumatic thing conspired by her mother. She was jealous of Rena's connection to her mother and she despised Rena anyway.

It was not her fault her parents were who they were and did whatever they did. Rena was pure at this point and genuinely was seeking someone to just love and accept her. She did not deserve Franklin's mother treating her so evilly and causing such malice and more trau-matic episodes for Rena.

Things did not work out as Rena thought life was meant to be, as Fredrick's mother had different plans for him even though the blood test show him 99.996% the father. She did not want her son with such an impoverished ward of the state such as Rena. Rena did spend her childhood from house to house in the system. Yet, as an adult that woman should have known better. Can a nine-year-old determine where she should live or if a parent is fit to raise her or not? Then to be tossed about was due to Rena's anger that no one sought help for or tried to figure her out.

Moreo had other plans for himself he was gonna show the world how great he is through his career and social status achievements. He rose to the top of every sport he participated in. If it was track or ball he was determined to excel. He was also, pretty darn good with those books. He would show his mother that "he was the son she should have never walked away from." Oh yes, she would surely need him before he needed her.

He graduated high school then college with a degree in psychol-ogy. He was married to his third girlfriend in life and for him life was awesome until he joined the Army. That's when the loyalty and fidelity of wives are really challenged. Some would say it was like being married to a man in prison. The only difference is separate rations. Throughout time Moreo found himself on wife number three and baby number two and in despair at wife number three truly not being a good match for him after all, and his heart was failing him for his search for love.

Rena went through many lessons along her rugged and some-times self laid brick road up life's highway. She married a soldier who she knew was heaven sent but, it was only after heartbreak and divorce number three she realized it was no man she or anyone else could do for her if she did not internalize a deep love for God in her-self and everyone else around her. She had been practicing now for fifteen years and had been tested on so very many levels. That's when she heard about it.

Moreo was coming to the states after being gone for six months and she had really been forward with him intimately unlike she had ever behaved in his presence. He didn't know what to think about it. She seduced him thinking she had to bond with him. She had to let him see and feel her on a deeper level. He had heard things bad things about Rena that no longer existed in her nature as he knew her to have grown to be. They kept a relationship as friends throughout life via the phone and internet. He was nervous the way he cut Rena off completely after their one night together. Rena told him she just wanted to treat him as if he was truly her husband for just that night.

She did and Moreo noted why her ex's wanted her back and that she made him feel more love and attention in one night than all his wives ever did. This is when she first spoke of soulmates and twin flames to him. Moreo told her he used to believe and that he thought his wife April was his soulmate. He told her he no longer believed and that it was not biblical anyway. He said it in such a condescending way if Rena didn't hear his soul over his big headed stubborn mouth, she would not have told him "Moreo you know I'm your soulmate quit playing" Moreo hung up and eventually blocked Rena on every level of communication. The only time she heard his voice from that moment on was when he would call ranting because he was aggravated with a situation, he didn't want to talk with Rena about.

The thing about it was Rena knew exactly what is was. She is spiritually connected to him on levels he has not understood yet. That night she saw it all. He was in a tug of war in his head, heart, and soul. Moreo loved the woman he was married to. Although he knew exactly who Rena is, he had found someone he treasured, and he was losing her and there was nothing he could do. She wanted to be free and the more he fought to keep her the more she turned into something he began to despise. He could also hear Rena's lonely heart and sweet prayers calling out to God and Galaxies. The Universe was tugging on him to be done with this painful cycle and return to that which he has known to be true always. Rena, the first girl to lock eyes with him ever and he felt her somehow, and knew she would be forever a part of his journey called life. He had this discovery at the ripe old age of twelve.

At this point in Rena's life she had to make some extreme eccentric choices in order to survive the life's fate she brought upon herself. She had created a criminal background with her anger and rage and now jobs for her were scarce and if they hired her on a level she could not move up. If she did and the promotion requires a background check, she would be released.

So, she depended heavily on God and the Holy Spirit to guide her some people call it intuition or instinct. Rena just obeyed the unctioning within in her. She always saved her money up to purchase big because of her job situation she could not have reoccurring debts.

After so very many years of working two, three, and four jobs and giving birth to seven children, fighting cancer three times Rena just wanted to raise her children in peace. She knew what homelessness felt like and she did her best to never allow her children to be homeless.

She saved her money to buy a foreclosed fixer upper with very few funds to fix her up with. Rena knew she would have to put her elbow grease into this project as well as hire some help. Her first round of help would destroy her dream, almost as if Satan himself came in disguised as a human and gutted her bathroom floor, took the main beam out so, the roof would sink. Rena was petrified, horrified, and vengeful but she only kept his tools and would not allow him back on her private property ever again. This put Rena in a deep depression internally that no one on her outside but her children who may have heard her sobbing in her pillow at night knew about. Rena only did the bare necessities to get by she had no inspiration. The house began to cover in soot from their heating source and she would not dust. She barely cooked so there were no dishes they were all dirty it was a mess.

Years went by and finally the twins father Rena's second husband contacted them four months before their eighteenth birthday to tell Rena about some money for the girls and for her doing such a great job with them that she deserved help. Well, after eight years and four months of struggling alone with the children she could use the money to strengthen and secure the house more so the twins would always have a home but also the others since Rena did purchase the home herself it was perfect timing because Rena was ready to travel and the twins would be the right age to do so.

Rena started looking for help to do her new remodeling campaign and her search lead her to Marvin and Christine, Moreo's mom and her lifelong companion. Marvin was super with carpentry and he did not charge Rena as much as someone else would have for the job he did. He agreed to her price and then he and Christine went above and beyond what she expected.

Rena just wanted warmth and security for her children and home. She had promised the girls before they left home she would have the work done and even she was beginning to doubt it and look at God. This was not a huge settlement, but it did secure the home and seal off holes that tormented them every winter. Now they were safer and warmer than they had been in the past four years and this sparked a light in Rena like she had not had in years.

Although she still suffered from separation anxiety and wonder of what's going to happen with her life now that she had no children to raise and no husband to care for what now? Then she hears Moreo is returning. She had been blogging for about a month now and landed a few writing gigs one of which she felt was sure to be her big break finally. She knew if this would happen not only would her immediate family be blessed by her rising, but many others that's just who she is. Even when she suffered single parenthood without help, she would help others and sometimes it would be couples. So she knew she mothered all people and nothing would have any affect against that. She and God had a love affair through her treatment of humanity and Rena was fully aware of this duty and she wore it like breathing. Because to Rena her breath was God's.

Moreo was nearing his divorce just as this story picks up, he had finalized it and he blocked Rena because he did not want her to follow his progress either way. If he had won Denya back he could just move on as if that night with Rena never happened and hope Rena found someone new, or he if could find no hope left in this situation and run back to Rena apologize explain his thinking and ask her to marry him and make him the blessed man he knows she would. The later happened the more he tried Denya got more disrespectful. She no longer loved him. He was a great provider and she knew that. She wanted some of his bank account to be transferred to hers. So without him knowing she only returned to try and catch him doing wrong. His good behavior and love and adoration to her was nothing but a weak pathetic cry out from a man who burnt her last nerve and her disdain for him she lost control of hiding, and the divorce was imminent as they had it scheduled already and were using this time to try and heal what can never be healed again. It was over. He was confusingly happy.

He needed to get his money together and enough to marry Rena bring her back to Germany with him and his children and give her and himself a good life. But what if he had said way too much to hurt Rena? He was very harsh and in reality, he did it in his own mind as a way to shut her completely off from feeling anything for him. He did not want her hurt and longing for him while he was in such a state of confusion. No, he would intentionally be hurtful. Yet, in his soul he wanted her to be there when it all came crashing down. Now, he didn't feel pain from he and Denya's divorce as he expected, she made darn sure of this with her behavior. His heart, mind, and soul knew Rena was the one, but he had been so brutal after finding out physically she was the one, what if she has totally given up?

He was determined to give love one more try even if not for his own sake alone, but for Rena as well. If we belong together, then we must do this now, so we have time to enjoy the end of our youth together at least. Moreo was frantic as the time lead up to his plane's departure date a month from now in December 2018.

Holiday Season 2018

Moreo rushed to finish his paperwork, he went into work every weekend leading up to his long-awaited return to the states. It's not that he hasn't been home to visit since being stationed in Wolfsburg Germany. But, for the first time he was returning to propose to the very first girl that ever made his heart feel alive. She was thirteen years old, and he was twelve then. Now, Moreo is approaching fifty fast and so is Rena. Rena is the love of Moreo's life, and he knew it light years before Rena ever got a clue. Which is not normal in the love zone. The bible says that God told Eve her desire would be unto her husband, so why didn't Rena desire me, Moreo pondered deep within. He loved God and his word, and as he grew in age and stature, he began to model his life to a picture he believed God would smile upon, and Rena is just the same. So maybe I'm wrong, Moreo concluded, and married another and Rena the same

Memories of Moreo:

"Rena, child, where have you been?" her mom asked, as she walked through the door exhausted from work.

"Hi mom," Rena retorted. "I'm not feeling too good mom. It's Moreo, he's coming to the states next month or so for the holidays. I'm not sure how it's going to go the last time he came; I manipulated the situation to force a bond with him. Because I know we are twin flames, but all it did was force him to shut me out of his life, and it hurt me as if we had been together, together. I mean yes, we've been friends our entire lives but somehow I have missed signals somewhere. I always thought we were strictly friend zoned, although deep in my heart he has never left my spirit, since I mistook him for a boy who grabbed my butt and ran. Hey, when I turned around, Moreo was the one standing there so I mushed him hard down to the ground. I think about it now, and it makes me sad. I want to go back and kiss that little boy and be his lifelong sweetheart and eternal soulmate. But, that's impossible. Mom look, the time he came to visit me in Brownvikch, and he was returning to the state's then as well," he said "Rena, I will be stopping by your house for some good old cooking and maybe hang out with you in your town a bit". Mom, I did not have a clue how a seed of love could be planted then. Moreo is sexy and desirable but, I respect and revere him so much so I would never be forward with anything, without first knowing he's interested in me in that way as well and since he never used words to guide me in any direction I kept everything in, until July and I just really mishandled that situation completely. I'm hoping and praying Moreo will at least let me see him during this holiday if he comes. During our phone call last night he mentioned he may or may not get to come to our home state, that he really doesn't come here. I missed it all mom, he only came for me twice, and I didn't, me, bright, witty, intellectually sound, analytically calculated Rena, never had a clue. His love was hidden right before my eyes.

"Rena baby you had to live through what you lived through, to become you, and you the Rena, my baby standing before me, are a rarity amongst humanity Rena I mean amongst humanity, not just amongst women baby. You're a rare find in the world, you're unbelievable baby, your pureness in spirit, love, and truth. I believe Moreo knows this is the right God given divine timing. If I am in God's spirit as I know I am I predict wedding bells in the near future."

"Mom, no don't do that," Rena said, pessimistically and secretly hopingly; I just really, really hope to get to see him. I mean to talk to him, to feel him alive and well on U.S. soil breathing and smiling, alive, and healthy and here with me. Me having a chance to see his eyes alive every so often makes my world okay.

Moreo's Flight and Surprise Landing:

Moreo prepared himself for a turbulent flight as it was a blizzard rising, exiting this old Germanic airport.

"Sheesh it's freezing back here" a lady yelled from behind Moreo's head, forward toward the bulkhead.

Moreo stood up to remove an extra wool blanket he packed for his trip. Placing the blanket across the lady securing the fabric in place for purpose of warmth. He smiled, thinking of Rena, she has no clue how dearly I love her. She has always been a necessary part of my humanity. Every divorce; all three, Rena was there in my corner cheering for me, uplifting me explaining how I am good and worthy of love, joy and happiness, I dare not rebuke her, for leaving me to these other women, because she overlooked me blindly and I too became bitter and vengeful and took her offer of love as a puny gesture of fleshly weakness, and a bit too little too late. I showed her; I blocked her butt on pictureme, hookedup, and speedtalk. I refused to answer any of her phone calls on a line I got specifically to communicate with her, and I am still keeping that phone active to this day. At first it was to hear her be in the same pain I felt she projected upon me by ignoring my love style, but then it became a door of promise to let her know I will always be here and I would never truly let her completely go. I'm her knight in shining armour, and I am heading inbound to get you my beautiful flower.

Twenty hours later the landing was smooth, Moreo was thrilled no jet lag in sight. Oh God be with me, this is the day I have written about, prayed for, and now at last dear God stay near and guide me. The Uber pulls up and Moreo palms began to drench. Wow, I just spent fourteen hours on a plane not including layovers and weather delays, ok Moreo it's time, don't stop anywhere before you get to Rena's house it is imperative that you do this right away.

This ride should only take forty-five minutes but, it seems like hours no, days the driver smells horrible, the music is loud, cars are zooming by, Oh God I'm getting sick. I'm nauseous.

"Stop the car," Moreo yelled, "I can't go a second farther. " Moreo jumped out the car and hurled. The driver questioned him twenty-one questions until he diagnosed Moreo and gave him a remedy.

"Get in the car my boy" the driver spoke with a loud and heavy Creole accent. He seemed to drive faster, getting to Rena's house in seconds. The driver was the hero, he just got out the car knocked on

Rena's door and when she opened the door Moreo could see her hair all tangled and all in disarray. The driver said, "there is a very, very sick man in the back of my car and he says God told him to have me drive him here to you ma'am, is your name Rena?" Rena answered, yes, it is as she reached for shoes and a jacket to go see about the matter and how she could be of help.

Moreo humped himself over to get in the role the driver had masterfully laid before him. Rena approached the door to which the driver was reaching. A man fell out of the backseat all balled up, he must be in severe pain.

"Oh No" Rena thought, I have got to help him. "God give me strength to lift him up to see what is here before me" she panted out.

As she proceeded to help the man into a better position for examining her patient, he leaped up to one knee, with a smile so bright eyes filled with so much adoration and pure love, "Marry Me Rena!" he said, "make me the happiest man to exist in time."

"YES, YES, YES, Moreo I do, I mean I will" she belted out right before she felt very flushed, weak in her knees, and fainted.

Yes, good old Moreo, our knight in shining armour caught her and walked her inside to process the joy they both had, now seen, had always been, and now is found!

The merging of two lifestyles: Moreo & Rena's journey

Religious Beliefs

Sunday mornings at the Ellroy house was not exactly how Moreo envisioned his happy life with his lovely new bride Rena would be. Rena was always dragging her feet, moving slow, and somewhat deliberately, Moreo thought to himself, with the passing of each Sunday. She was causing him and the children to show up for service later and later by the week. Once at church, Moreo noticed his beauty never followed with the hymnals nor the responsive reading portion. Although she very much seemed to be engulfed in the praise and worship section of service. This was the only time, he noticed, she was present at any point during service.

Moreo grew up Southern Baptist, and that's what he knows. He believed in the Bible and he loved God with all of his heart, mind, body, and soul. He, cringed to think of a possibility that the woman he loves and hails second only to God, did not know God or have a personal relationship with God. Moreo pondered, " If you're listening, God, how could I have fallen for a woman so far from your spirit?" Moreo approached the pulpit during the alter call and Rena stayed back in her seat as the children filed out of their pew row, stepping on her sore feet and scuffing her brand new shoes to go stand with their dad for prayer. Rena silently squatted in her pew knees on the floor and covered her head turning toward the east respectfully in the direction of Mecca, Israel, and the rising of the Sun. She prayed very silently although her lips were moving, no one could hear her petition unto God.

After service ended, Moreo decided to invite his wife and children out for a late lunch, early dinner treat. Rena agreed quickly, as she had not prepared Sunday dinner. That was another thing that bothered Moreo. "I'm used to my home smelling like heaven on

Sundays, and my wife, just would truly prefer to lay around, read, take walks in nature and feed all the animals she has collected." He thought to himself, but he never spoke to Rena of it, since she was an excellent cook and provided three hot meals for him and the children Monday through Saturday. "She's amazing." He wondered in agony what spirituality her allegiance was truly to.

They had had the basic conversations on religion and politics, and as far as politics go, Rena had no position and refused to take one, "Jesus bore the government on his shoulders" she would say, "It is God who sets up Kings and it is God who tares them down, I am only bothered by a king when his rules reach out to the poor folks lifestyles, and for as long as I have lived nothing a king has done has trickled down far enough that I have seen my community drastically benefit from or hugely suffer from. I trust that God will allow whoever will, carry out each phase of HIS Sovereign mission one term at a time, in the mean time, I must carry out my sovereign mission to wife, nurture, and cover you and these children God has so graciously blessed me to have in my life today."

Look Deeper, Moreo

Gold Carroll's was crowded today as always, but the food was good, and the prices were reasonable. Moreo could take his entire four-man crew here every day to eat no problem. That's what he had been doing for a year or so before Rena. Rena, he looked across the table at this outstanding gorgeous woman, who is now all his, like he'd been dreaming since middle school. But, in his heart he turned over thoughts that drove him secretly mad inside. "really God," he thought, "the woman I love and adore so much, she is highly regarded in every form of charity and philanthropy, and to no avail if she doesn't truly know you. God, I want my dear sweet wife to join you and I in heaven, together in your home of glory. I don't want to ever be without her again in this life or the next."

Moreo jerked himself out of thought to look across at Rena playing with his children as her own, and she loves them like she birthed them, no one knew from looking at them from the outside, she was the stepmom. Especially with Moreo, Jr. She was the answer to his prayers, because of Rena he was home with his dad in a safe stable environment and she was kinda cute but very helpful with school work and she played his video games almost as good as he. Jr. Loved Rena. Mariam, loved her as well, being that Rena entered their lives at a pivotal point in her teenage life, boys, classes, girls teasing her about being a late bloomer, braces on her teeth and more, besides her mom mistreating her for being a dead ringer for Moreo, Rena thought she was absolutely gorgeous and spent genuine time teaching Mariam this loving truth, one day at a time.

Rena's truth that balances the scales

Coming back home from Gold Carroll's was loud and cheery and that was thanks to Rena, everyone in the car felt blessed to have her there. Rena was blessed to have them as well. After all her children where grown, she had feared facing life alone. No one in the home besides her, or she may get a visit on the holiday, or when she's babysitting grands, but that rarely happened now that the grands are in school. Although Rena is only a year older than Moreo her children were much older than his. Her baby was in college. Rena had been married and divorced three times as had Moreo. Rena started life at a much younger age than Moreo did so, she was done rearing children when she and Moreo connected. Rena new in her soul she loved Moreo because he is the only man on God's good green earth she would give more of her life energy to assist in rearing children.

After the children were bedroom bound. Rena walked into the study where Moreo goes to look at catalogs of weapons and ammunition and place orders via the computer. He has a heavy job order being in charge of hundreds of troops and keeping them battle ready with weapons and training. Rena understood all too well her position of keeping Moreo stress free and at ease. She knew something was spiritually nagging her lord king and she wanted to clear any confusion he may have, Rena was born with what the old folk would call a cull or vail over her face. It is said to be because the child was born directly from the fifth dimension sent for a specific curse breaking mission. Moreo had no clue of this, because Rena always felt awkward when it came to her full self-expression around Moreo, she didn't want to disturb any of his peace. She adored him and she knew she loved the right God or she would never be here with Moreo (the man she'd written about fasted for and prayed for) she would still be in the States and quite possibly in the state of the people who lack God in their lives there, on drugs, killing, robbing, and hustling one another. Although an Orphan and troubled teen and young adult Rena knew God from age four because of her Bigmama and she never let Gods hand go throughout life and with time her personal relationship with God became more important than anything else in life including breathing.

Rena Speaks Truth

Being highly intuitive and empathetic Rena was drawn to the issue of Moreo's heart, she gently grabbed his hand away from the keyboard and placed it on her heart. She looked deep into his eyes, Moreo shifted a little from the fierce intent behind his love bugs eyes. He had never seen Rena look so fiery. She must mean what she's about to say to me, I better brace myself mentally.

"Geesh I need a glass of water" Moreo stood up quickly heading toward his mini fridge in the study. Rena smiled they are so spiritually connected it's ridiculous how long it took Moreo to fuse this love union.

Rena started, "Moreo, you know I love you correct?"

He answered, "yes."

"I also know you more than you are aware, dear husband. I'm your rib and therefore I am privy to feel some of what you feel and especially spiritual things like my connection to source."

Moreo spewed water everywhere. Rena giggled in her knowing and continued as she grabbed Moreo's hand and walked him out the side patio door, exiting the study; to a view over the mountains.

Godly Revelation

"Sweet husband," Rena stated, "look at these mountains how sure and certain are they, look at the water banking against the mountain how so not intimidated is the ocean by the great mountain. For although the ocean is beneath the mountain the ocean can swallow the mountain whole, for us to never see it above sea level again. This is the beauty and fierce power of God. You see that sky, how it reflects everything on earth and in the galaxies the perfect blue, although we are taught all colors reflected make black. You see the trees, all in their green glory with their contribution of food and oxygen to man. In each tree's due season it shall provide food, or shade, oxygen and remove carbon dioxide emissions from the airways to keep us flowing free. That is God."

She let his hand go and began to twirl across the field atop the mountain where they stood.

She said, "The rains come in scheduled timing it's scheduled to come when God says so, the wind blows only because God says so, the ocean, it knows how far to come inland because it obeys God and his word, the birds awake singing praises to God daily, and no one has to witness it. There is a melody that plays in my heart that reminds me, that the earth is God's and the fullness there of; and everything that has breath must praise the Lord." She twirled until she felt dizzy, and as she was to tumble Moreo was there to bare most of the fall. She fell into his arms.

She looked into his eyes and asked him, " Moreo, do you believe I love you?"

"Yes." he answered without hesitation.

"Then how is it possible for you to believe undoubtedly that I love you, and yet worry of my connection to God. Moreo, there's no form of love absent of God. God is love and in love he created all things and without love nothing was created. These that are devoid of love suffer a fate I wish not upon my worse enemy, if I had enemies." She went on to speak of God's love, twirling around again.

"Rena" Moreo thought. "We are too old to be falling down", he chuckled inside, and stayed very close to his free-spirited bride.

"Moreo, she giggled, "For God so loved the world, that he gave his only begotten son, that whosoever believeth in him should not perish, but everlasting life. Moreo, I love God but, I don't believe it to be expressed as we were taught growing up. The wild beastly open displays that resemble demonic possession, and so not the gentle precious holy spirit. " They both fell this time. She went on, "Or how about traditions that give no honor to God but to consumerism. Moreo I don't care for churches because I grew a bad taste in my mouth for the message of prosperity and many other non Christ related doings, but I am here with you in Germany attending church submitting to your rule over me. I am a child of the Most High Creator God the only one true living God and you are second to him only. Jesus Christ is my savoir and redeemer, yet, I must work out my soul's salvation with fear and reverence. My love I'm always concerned with all the secular activities going on in and about the church, but I never fear your stance with our God and Creator, I never question it because I know I am plugged into the right source, and I was lead to your safety." She kissed his ring finger and stood up.

Moreo's Heart Is Eased

"Rena!" Moreo exclaimed, as he jumped to his feet. "Marry me and make me the happiest man to exist in my time."

"Uuhm, Moreo, we did that part already, that's why we are here."

"No, Rena" he pleaded, " I want you to walk an aisle, you deserve it, the right way, (knowing she never had a gown or bouquet) I want to be standing in wait for my bride to be handed to me like God handed Eve to Adam. I know both our father's are dead but, you have a son old enough to be your dad."

He giggled at his joke about her youngest son, she giggled cause her baby boy does act like an old man, she rolled her eyes and Moreo started tickling her, she yelled out "Old Bladder" and they both hollered out laughing. Moreo went right back to topic, "Rena it can be as big as you like or as cozy as you'd like but I want to give this to you."

Rena truly wanted this as well, as she always dreamed of a church wedding, but her marriages were all handle by the magistrate and Moreo is offering her dream. He was her dream man, and now making both their dreams come true.

The merging of two lifestyles

The journey of Moreo and Rena; Merging Families and family values:

March was approaching quickly, which meant May was not too far away. Rena walked into the study where Moreo was working intensively to get ration and artillery orders in, and his monthly report out, by an unspecified to Rena, deadline. Rena paused at the door to stand and gaze a while at Moreo. It had only, yet already been four wonderful months of wedded bliss. He is so intelligent handsome, sexy, strong and knows the word of God like he knows the back of his hand. She looked at his back and shoulders and thought a silly little dirty thought. He's her husband and if his shoulders turn her on, well who can be her judge? Just then Moreo turned around. He looked so beautiful to Rena, she honored him as the royal son of God that he is and Moreo honored her as a godly and virtuous woman, and when he looked at her, Rena could get lost in his dreamy eyes, filled with what she felt to be adoration for her. It made her feel like God loved her and treasured her among all women, to bless this angelic man with her, as his reward for a job well done in his life, to help him meet the rest of the goals God has for them both.

"Come in dear" Moreo waved to his wife for her to come near.

"Hey babe" Rena said. "Do you know how much longer you will need for work? I have to speak with you about my trip back to the states in May."

Moreo shifted uncomfortably in his deluxe model recliner, swiveling, rocking, leather, rolling desk chair. Yep, the chair is all that and then some. That is why Moreo had it, it helped to relieve pressure from pivotal points on the body which prevent compilation of multiple stresses to his mind and body at once. Moreo was super smart he needed that chair. Nothing but the best for Moreo. Rena got it for him when she saw it at Brecks, an upscale furniture store that sales one-time productions only, when they went shopping back around the holiday season.

"Rena" Moreo started, "what are you talking about, your trip to the states? What trip to what states, and for what?" He asked with a straight confused look on his face.

"Moreo", Rena paused and looked at his eyes to see how he was receiving the message as she began to speak. "My daughter is graduating from college in May remember?"

"Yeah, so, what am I going to do with my children while you go off to the states, and how am I to know you would really come back over here to us, if you go there without us? I refuse, Rena, I can not allow you to go. That is my final stance on the matter and don't try to sway my hand."

He stood up and walked over to Rena and kissed her cheek, grabbing her hand placing it over his heart, he said looking through her pupils directly into her soul, "Rena, there is no way I will ever live another day without you. You know it is too short of a notice for me to place a request order for time off to go to the states, especially this soon after the holiday season and plus I had to pay for four tickets back here to have my whole family with me. Baby I can't let you go alone what if you don't make it back to me? Rena I'd die." He teared up and his voice cracked, unlike the Moreo Rena knew. But she always knew he was human with real feelings and emotions, so it didn't perplex her too much.

"Moreo" Rena whined as she walked away from him facing the beautiful mountainside, outside his patios sliding glass doors. She placed her hand bare against the glass as to be connecting with a source of strength to come fuel her with surety to speak her truth to Moreo, she never felt this hurt and angry with her lord king about any final decisions he had ever made before. "Moreo" she started again, "You, sir are jumping to conclusions twice when you first, think I am asking you to pay for the ticket to and from the states, second because you think there is something I would rather do than to return to you and my babies."

"We aren't your babies" Mariam swung the door open so hard the knob hit the wall leaving an impression. "Let her go dad, if she don't want to be here with us, we got us like always, I got Jr. after school while you work and Gold Carroll's is our first mom anyway, so we gone eat without her."

"Huh? "Rena said feeling so not aware of what was going on at this moment. She thought to herself "God show me my seven ways out of this spiritual trap Satan is trying to weave here to destroy my family, Holy Spirit lead me now guard my tongue so that peace may abound."

Just then, Jr. walked in, and at one glance he summarized exactly what was going on in the room plus he could hear a huge bit of it from down the hallway in his bedroom. It was surely a heated first. He looked toward his dad and sister then, toward Rena and walked toward her with a face as being prepared to plead. Jr. grabbed Rena's sleeve and said, "Rena would you like to go play a video game?"

"Sure Jr." Rena answered.

Jr. was a lot more receptive than most eight-year-olds, and much wiser, almost a miniature adult lol. "Rena," said Jr. "I don't want to play a game, I want to tell you something. Rena, are you coming back to us after you see your daughter graduate?"

"Yes Jr." Rena said as her heart began to hear a story coming, she may feel some empathy for.

"Rena, dad never had a woman like you, that wants him happy and healthy and you let him be silly and crazy and you still love him cause y'all act just alike. Me and Mariam always talk about what it would have been like had we been born from you and dad and your other children as well, like we are, your babies in chronological order Mariam would be number eight and I would be number nine and y all would call me Nine for my nickname that would be so cool right Rena?"

"Oh yes baby but, we can not redo what is already done and can

20

not be undone, like typing a text but not hitting send yet."

"Rena, Dad is scared you won't come back that some man may be waiting for you to return to the states and swoop you up off your feet like a Prince charming. My sister, she's his protector, Mariam is not like a naggy daddy's girl and don't want dad to be loved by any woman but her mom, nope she prefers dad's happiness over everybody, because dad does everything to make sure the people he loves are happy, and we have seen women drag our dad's heart for money any other stinky grown old people stuff. Anyway, I know you love us and you're coming back, they don't. So, I brought you in my room cause you needed your team too."

Rena busted out in tears, what little Moreo had said made perfect since and tonight she and the precious spirit bestowed upon her just for Moreo from the Most High was going to help her reassure him of her love in this matter.

Rena wiped her face, "Sorry Jr." she said.

"For loving us Rena? No, don't be sorry for that. I'm on your side okay? Me you and God! I'm going to pray for dad's trust muscles to grow stronger just for you Rena. I trust you."

Rena started tickling Jr. "What do you know of the woes we adults have with trust?"

Jr. laughed and howled so loud he brought his dad and sisters attention to his bedroom door where they found a scene of Rena picking Jr. up scuffing him on top his head and sitting him on her lap as she sat on the edge of his bed and she spoke.

"Listen Moreo, Jr. I am not going anywhere ever from you, your sister, or your dad unless it be God's will through death. Do you understand?"

"Yes" Jr. replied. She continued, you may or may not be too young to understand this being you're already a fifty-five-year-old," they both chuckled. "I have loved your dad since I was younger than your sister. He was one of the little dudes in school and cute as could be, plus he was always quiet and to himself mostly unless his boys were around. He seemed to always be thinking about something sad but, I had a lot of sad things going on at home as well. I moved away from that school and soon found out I probably would not be returning to that school district ever, because I would be permanently placed in my grandparents' home in Cloverland so that was it no more Moreo unless wishing on stars will bring him to my school," she giggled. "That never happened and the we lost touch for many, many years and one day I was trying a new social networking site and your dad's name was in the top listed as one of the people I may know. I'm not sure who requested who or how it happened but somehow the heavens had led him to find me and I will confess I was confused why so many years, children, marriages, and emotional scars later, so I decided it must be because he was trying to reach out to old classmates and have spots to go when he is in the states, and for me, Moreo is welcome where ever I am"

"Eww" Jr. said "stop the googly eyes."

"What googly eyes? "Rena asked jokingly, as she tickled him with one hand while holding him close and firm so he couldn't jerk out of her grip with the other.

"The wan wan wan googly eyes you make when you say dad's name, or look at him, I be peeping out everything." He said knowingly.

Rena laughed and said, "Well big guy how are we gonna get dad and Mariam on our side?"

"Your side?" Moreo interrupted, "Rena are you mad? Do you think for second that talking to an eight-year-old little boy will give you the rocket fuel you're gonna need to break my will? Girl you must be out of your ever-loving mind."

"Girl?" Rena thought to herself,"girl? Moreo, really?"

After the children were in bed Moreo took a cot from the outside storage unit and bedding into his study. Rena just followed him around silently praying in her spirit. "God please hear me now, I need you to show up mighty and strong." She walked off into their bedroom still talking, and fell on her knees at the end of the shrunk Moreo purchased from Brecks as well during the holiday season, it was very elegant and like something Rena only dreamed of owning before Moreo. She prayed aloud now, "God please hear me your worthy bonded servant, help me with my dear husband Moreo." Due to paranoia he stood silently listening to her from beside the door, just in case she decides to call on a man besides God he wanted to be right there to bust her whole plan up. Rena spoke softly to God as a child humbles her spirit before her parents when begging, "Father what is this, you gave me to this man not showing him I'd be after his very heart? Or is it he does not see that for scars? How is this your will that he takes something that means so much to my family dynamics away from me and he knows not about the things I promised my children for peace sake to be here with him and his children. I'm already separating the house when I must pray for help with judgement on his and my children. Moreo is placing me in a position that tests me and my position with my children and you, as well as himself. Father I am sure what I am to do and with a humble heart I accept my position as Moreo's help meet and if he is not ready for me to leave his side comfortably then , God my God forsaking all others, I stand with my love in my honor to you and I ask you to give me the words to say to my child so she will not feel abandoned nor resent my husband. Amen." She ended her prayer and immediately grabbed her cell phone.

"Exactly" Moreo thought, he was just about to repent until she grabbed that cell, "women," he thought.

"Hello?" Rena always had her phone on speaker phone so it was up loud, and Alexis' voice rang through it caught him totally off guard she was calling her daughter. "Hi Alexis," Rena struggled. "Baby I don't think there will be a way for me to make it to your graduation baby."

"Mom" Alexis interrupted.

"Yes, Pooh?"

"Mom you're married and by the ordinances you raised me to

observe as being set by God when you left, I was pleased with why you would not be at my graduation, you finally got Mr. Moreo. Mom, I of all your children know your plight for this man, and if God saw you worthy enough to give this man's heart to you, baby girl I'm twenty-four and my mama raised a royal priestess and I know what's up. Stay and love your new starting family whole, y'all just better come to my wedding when I drag Keyshore to this alter."

She giggled so hard Rena forgot why she was nervous, she raised excellent children off pure love and Godly principles so why would Alexis think her mom would be there? What could make Rena assume her child would not be led of the same spirit she was reared in? Rena laughed at Alexis's joke and said, "girl that boy been dragging himself behind you like a lost puppy for nine years when are you going to be his bride?"

"Soon mom, Alexis shared, soon I graduate soon and that's a big milestone after highshool, college graduation then he can propose again and I swore to God on my eyes I will say yes, I just didn't need the love and relationship distractions during school now, I am ready, mom I gotta go, I love you kiss my dad, sis, and bro for me, I love you later!" Rena could hear noise growing in Alexis background just before she hung the phone up.

"Well," Rena thought out loud. "thank you, God, for your precious Holy Spirit teaching me how to raise my children, I don't think my having a man in the home physically would have helped me produce that better than you and I."

Moreo stepped in but not in the steed he pictured himself barging in like before her sweet prayer and revelation of raising God fearing and order acknowledging children such as she had.

"Rena I am so very sorry for being so crazy with you earlier, how can I make it up to you? You deserve the heavens my dear and if I could posses them, I would bundle them up and tie it with a bow just for you Rena."

Rena kissed Moreo and said, "how about some bedroom chacha

hehehe" she giggled so hard cause Moreo always forgot a step and ended up naked well before she did. She wasn't sure if he lost on purpose or if he really had no rhythm. It never mattered to her either way, whoever gets naked first is the others love slave and Moreo played that role well. He was her undercover bad, bad boy and she loved it!

"You're stuck with me Moreo, you and my babies I'm not going anywhere until I'm not breathing, you got me?" She asked with authority as she switched the lights off before he could answer, diving under the covers, "Moreo?"

"Yes Rena" she bit him on the ear lobe and repeated "You're stuck with me, no givesie backsies, you got me?" "Yes, Rena baby I got you and I am more than blessed."

Financial Stability

Back in the states the holiday season was just about to kick off. Rena imagined what her favorite bath spray store had her hometown shopping mall smelling like right about now. " Eww pumpkin spice, yuck" she thought and giggled to herself.

Since joining her family here in Germany, she found it awfully amusing how the Germans seem to find any day a reason to be celebratory as well as drunk she giggled at her thought.

Last month there was " United European Day" October seventh was " Harvest of Festivals" day, tomorrow is "Halloween" which Rena didn't celebrate at all, nor any of the rest. She thought on the fact the Germans having so very many pubs, nearly every corner was hosted by a sports bar.

She relished, to think of what the celebration of November first was about the "Night of Broken Glass." Could it have been riots and looting going on hopefully they aren't celebrating pillage and plunder.

She would not be the judge she would simply just be Rena and not acknowledge nor participate in that which does not lead to becoming more godly. As she dusted the decorative mantle piece facing the street side of their spacious condo home, she was startled by the appearance of a what is known to her as a deputy sheriff.

"He must be at the wrong address." She thought, as he just stood there staring at her door and window as looking to make sure nobody moves before he approaches. A familiar silver car pulls up and parks alongside the deputy's vehicle. It was Tony, Moreo's favorite staff sergeant and long-time friend. Out of all of Moreo's sub department heads he gives Tony the most credit for why he Moreo was always at the top of his game and their company performed with such precision they are yearly recognized and awarded.

Rena moved quickly to the front door unlatching the storm door quickly to see the matter these two gentlemen were here to present.

Tony approached the first step, "Ma'am," he paused.

"Ma'am?" Rena thought puzzled by the look and tone Tony represented himself in.

"Ma'am," he started again, "the deputy here has a certified letter here addressed to you and your husband. "By law," he continued, "it must be signed at reception. It is my duty as representative of the United States Army, that all be in good interest of the enlisted party at hand to be present and encourage you to and witness reception of this letter with signature, on behalf of my commanding officer Corp. Moreo Ellroy." And with a salute and quick right flank he moved to allow the deputy entry to perform his task.

After diner Rena told Moreo of the letter, and he was eager to see what it could be about. So, after everyone was settled into homework for Jr. and Maraim was dropped off at her new part time evening job at the local movie theater, they sat snuggled on the two seater that was special to them alone, right by the decorative built in fire place in the glass wall overlooking part of the waters not hidden by the majestic mountains. It was one of Rena's most favorite places in the entire home.

She handed the letter to Moreo unopened. He read the sender information: "Department of Social Human Services Louisville, Kentucky" the hometown of Moreo Jr.'s mother, April. "Oh no" Rena thought to herself.

After opening the letter and carefully studying it, Moreo stood up, passed the letter to Rena and walked out of the living room toward his study.

She quickly unfolded the letter and skimmed it for que key words to help her understand her husband's response to what was written on the paper. He was being sued by April, she was accusing him of predivorce relations with Rena, (which could be unequivocally proven as falsity and delusion) and back child support on Jr. for the time he was off training away from home before he even knew Jr was in existence. He hasn't missed a breath of Jr.'s since he found out about him. So, why now? What's up?

Six months and two hundred forty-five thousand dollars later, April won the back child support and she was right about Moreo's infidelity but not with Rena, she had another **loss of affection** case on grounds of his relations with his previous ex wife, Mariam's mother which she had no problem proving in a dramatic concerta that had even Rena hurting a little.

Rena had been working now about three months with a young new caterer and she was loving it. She was back to work and in rare form. She had assembly skills, packing, shipping and receiving, and could she cook? was never the question. She and her new business partner Van, had a lucrative business in less than three weeks of opening, because they were consistent, timely, and the food was divine. Everyone they could handle definitely scheduled their parties with "Food by Design" and the sky was the limit. Rena was averaging twelve hundred weekly take home to the bank no problem.

Home life was always quiet and, she always made it home in time daily to cook diner, lay Moreo and Jr.'s night and next day clothes out. Mariam petty much handled all of her own dressing needs since she was also "swagger out" Rena never challenged it and learned a lot about her daughter's personality through her chosen gear ware.

Moreo noticed his beauty was going to bed much earlier than normal, and he could not shake the feeling, "she must be feeling I have failed. I have her way over here in another country, and we are broke. I'm broke busted and disgusted and we are now living paycheck to paycheck, something Rena never had to do even as a single mom with seven children" Moreo had thoughts playing in his mind that made him feel sick, less than a man, far from Rena's knight in shining armour. Nope, his past discrepancies had come from the darkness to shatter his dream of finally rescuing Rena from an undeserved life of suffering and poverty. What now? She won't even talk to him in the evenings after diner anymore.

Rena's new routine consisted of caring for the needs of her family after working a job she knew Moreo would never approve of. He was her superhero and he would go ballistic to know Lois Lane likes to work and can help make ends meet like nobody's business. HER bank account was brimming, and her family was well looked after, she just showered and went to bed shortly after. Although she loved her new calendar, she was pooped around eight-thirty, nine o'clock and out like a light.

"What is it?" Moreo wondered. "Has she grown tired with me? Am I not as appealing to her broken like this, by my actions with another marriage? Could it be she has found a secret lover? No," he threw that last thought completely out of his mind. Nope, not his Rena, and heaven itself would testify on her sweet righteous behalf, and he knew that with real assurity.

It was the end of the corporate fiscal year and Moreo was on base more and more even weekends, preparing for the yearly audit of his battalion that he commanded. It was surely a stress filled and seriously accountable time for Moreo as he was very strategic and meticulous with every civilian's penny spent under his direction. So, this led him to long work days and stretched office encounters.

After so many countless days of work Moreo's team convinced him to order food, by insinuating "filled bellies keep brains sharp." Some of the soldiers mentioned different places that catered and other random delivery spots. "Food by Design" winning unanimously for the word of mouth advertising and the curiosity for new cuisine. Tony called them up and placed the order. He was hungry and ready to grub as the others.

"Feed us, boss man," he said smiling with a twinkle in his eye that said "Fooood" in an imagined by Moreo, "Homer Simpson's" voice. Moreo laughed to himself at his friends' eyes having a voice.

After careful deliberation and saddening acknowledgment of not having enough help on hand to avoid having to personally deliver the orders to Moreo's company, Van agreed to Rena staying inside the delivery van in the driver's seat while she walked the food inside and wait for the payment and receipt.

It seemed like it was taking forever for Van to come back for the second load. Rena heard a familiar voice accompanying Van coming toward the vehicle. It was Moreo, good ole Moreo, he couldn't sit and allow Van to single handedly carry three hundred meals alone although her cart carried one hundred at a time. He brought his own that could handle at least fifty and that was some help. What he always intended to be at all times was useful and of some help under whatever circumstances. Although back home he felt very useless in his wife's bedroom.

Van started acting weird, she started getting rushy and pushy toward Moreo, she knew exactly who he was and refused to allow him to get chatty with her. But, to no avail, Moreo noticed it, he caught a whiff of Rena's perfume. It was definitely her scent; he drank it in at every exposure to his love that he could.

He walked to the driver's door and peered in and without a surprised look. But, a look of sheer disappointment.

Days went by without word of Rena's disloyalty to Moreo's rule. At last Moreo spoke to her in a voice of a broken man who has lost all authority and his total manhood. "Rena, I have failed you as a husband, protector, and provider."

"No, Moreo," she interrupted.

"Ah shhh," he replied. Placing his right index finger over his lips. "Rena do you remember how frustrating it was when you were not sure I would ever wake up and realize you were sent to me by God? Don't answer" he said quickly. Rena I was making sure everything was aligned properly so we could have a successful start to our happily ever after. I made you feel rejected, neglected, and abandoned because I didn't want to ask you to wait on me to clear everything up. I would be selfish. I just prayed that when my I's were all dotted and my t's all crossed that if you were who my soul told me you were then your soul would hold you still for me baby. That, you did, Rena you waited on me to be your "Romeo" and the past few months I have performed less than average on the man scale in my book. Then to find you working secretly behind my back as if I am a tyrant to whom you can't discuss your financial fears or needs with. What has this become? Am I not the man of your desire anymore or am I weak broke local joker you feel you gotta store a nest egg up just in case the entire bottom fell out. You being tired had me questioning our intimacy and my performance and even if you were attracted to me anymore. You're out here working a job and taking care of the home. Who exactly is the man here and why do you fear my ability to get us back in the black financially?"

Rena swallowed hard, it was like she was on trial prejudged. She thought a second on her words and the affect they would have on her sweet lover's psyche. She stood up and walked to the middle of the room where they were sitting as if she was about to give a lifelong dissertation. She spoke looking directly into the eyes of her audience (Moreo).

"Moreo, my love and lord, I am but a woman after my God's own heart before yours always my lord king. I dare not go against your rule unless lead by the spirit of the living God who resides within my heart. I can never say for once in any instance that I have thought you to be weak or lack power and authority. I am your true rib and I feel how you worry even in your sleep your breathing vibrates to my soul your plight.

"I, knowing you and your desire to keep me safe and our children covered without struggle, is my total motivation for not presenting my work opportunity to you for debate. I know you and your will. So, why try to hash out something you and I both agree you would have shut down immediately.

"Moreo you are my sexy, strong, warrior king and I want you around me for as long as time will allow. You being under your regular stresses and duties and this past year's upset, made me weary and afraid with your blood pressure situation. I can't lose you, who on earth would care for me then? Who Moreo? Who will love and protect and provide for me and the children if something should happen to you due to stress God forbid? No amount," she screeched out and teared up. She proceeded, " No amount of money or no house, car, bank account or heaven itself would soothe me after so many stars wished upon for this union with you dear husband. They may as well toss me in with you."

"I did this, not to betray you but to help you meet the goals God placed in your heart for our family. I already found Van an excellent replacement. I'm tired and too old for all I was doing she giggled, while rubbing her left shoulder."

She approached Moreo with an envelope in her hand and sat closely beside him as snug as she could get without sitting directly atop his lap. As she was beginning to hand him this very thick manila envelope she said, "I have been missing the bedroom cha cha and my sexy daddy love slave very much. Here's my dowry, consider it a consolation prize for getting stuck in the side with this lady right here, who claims she's your rib and help meet." She kissed him and said it's not a quarter million dollars it's only fifteen thousand and some change, to bank and have a better look on our future together."

Moreo looked at this amazing woman sitting beside him, **Outstanding** was it. That's it nothing less, outstanding. "Rena," he said. "I am heading to take a shower my dear, I hear there's a dancing damsel in distress in need of a partner to do the cha cha with!" He was undressing so fast; Rena thought he would surely slip at the speed he was heading toward that steaming shower. "Slow down lover boy," she said coyly with a wink.

Moreo yelled over the shower and the slow jam Rena had started playing in the background, "SOMEBODY IS DUUUUUE A CHA chaaaaah ahhhaaahaaha," (in his version of a man gone mad impersonation.)

Merging of two lifestyles - the journey of Moreo and Rena:

Dealing with Ex's (petty life)

"Yes!" everyone exclaimed at Moreo's announcement of their long-awaited trip back to the states. The joy he saw on his family's face filled his heart and he almost teared up. "Never" he thought "not today." He smiled at his family as they all were his hearts desire.

Rena was always in charge of planning, and scheduling, and the touring as Moreo expected of her. She was buzzing around humming and singing for the next hour or so. Within the week she had the flights to and from. She had scheduled to visit family members on their specific days off.

Rena had the hotel reserved and all the places to eat besides family members houses and cooking in the mini kitchen at the hotel. She even had schedules for the latest movies, and theme park bands on reserve. She was awesome. Moreo had nothing to worry about, but to love, protect, and keep her.

Finally, back in the good ole U. S. of A. "Dad, am I going to be with y'all or are you going to force me to go to her house?" asked Mariam.

"Your mother," Moreo paused. "She is your mother" he said with a slow deliberate tone, with a matter of fact sting on the end of it. Mariam glanced quickly at Rena in pity. She knew the affect her mom had on her dad, and they were in the states.

Rena went on through the door dividing the two rooms to check on Jr. He was sitting on the end of the bed with a sad concerned look on his face. "What is it Jr.?" Rena asked.

"Ah nothing much," he replied. "Just worried about you and dad and Denya."

"Well, don't you worry your sweet little head with such matters, me, dad, and God got this. I'm not worried about your dad and Denya one bit and you shouldn't either."

"Rena," said Jr. "you trust God for everything, and I pray you're right because I don't want dad to lose you like he lost my mom." I love you very much, Rena."

"God is, Jr. and I trust him and his presence in your dad and my-self." She walked out back into the side she and Moreo were sharing. Moreo was sitting on the edge of the bed watching football on the sports channel. He waved to Rena to join him. "Hey babe, how's it cooking good looking." He tickled her and kissed her forehead.

She sat next to him quietly and awaited the pizza she had ordered on her phone app from years before. "Thank God I still had the phone with the app" she thought to herself. " After twenty straight hours of travel there would be definitely no cooking, dining out, or much visiting this first day. No Rena made her family rest, eat, and make phone calls to family and friends to notify them of their safe arrival.

Day one plan worked well for Moreo. He sat like a little boy watching that t.v. screen as if he was fantasizing about running the ball back for the "touchdown" himself. He had his drink, his favorite lady by his side and his children were on the other side of the door safe. He was good and he was well aware of his blessed life and was grateful to God.

The pizza arrived just in time Jr. had only just come for the first time to report that he could hear his belly grumbling, and for that Moreo tipped the driver ten dollars, for the sake of peace. The driver thanked him and he shook his hand Moreo said "no man, thank you" and let the driver go.

"Ahh Papa Don's," Moreo and the children said at the same time. "How did you know this was my favorite, Rena?" Mariam asked.

"I didn't," Rena replied. "Papa Don's better ingredients better pizza" Rena quoted the commercial and she and Mariam cracked up laughing and high fived like girls had some secret intuition on good pizza.

"Yeah right" Moreo retorted. "Get on outta here Mariam with all that girl giggle powerfluff you and Rena hehehe self, the game is on." Jr. laughed so hard he had to run to the bathroom and yes, he repeated Moreo "Powerfluffs" over and over until he was singing it. Moreo cracked up laughing. "Forget this game he said let's just hang out and eat pizza," and that's exactly what the first day ended with, they all prayed together and said their good nights.

The next day started as if they were back home in Wolfsburg. Rena prepared breakfast, everyone showered, ate, and dressed for the day's events. Today would be about Rena's older children and family, as they had not all met Moreo, and none had met Mariam and Jr. There was a nervous excitement in the air.

As planned, they all gathered at the home Rena had purchased many years ago for her adult children to always have to fall back if life's going got rough. This place was extremely special to Rena and the shear foundation of her being the rock and matriarch of her family. The older children parked well in the back so to leave the drive open for their mother's arrival. "Such thoughtfully respectful children," Moreo thought to himself when he saw how courteous they were.

Once inside Tylaya and Milaya the twins and youngest of the older seven children greeted everyone with hugs and kisses, while taking their jackets and offering a place to sit. From the back there was a low rumble turning into a loud "Welcome Home" from the five oldest as they carried a large white sheet cake with Rena and Mariam's favorite icing whipped cream butternut. The twins just whisked poor little Mariam away like they had just won a prize real life diary that they would share their every thought with. She was excited for the ride they were taking her on. She listened to them attentively.

"We are grateful to God for your safe arrivals and we have prepared a bonding day," said the oldest of them all Frederick.

"Yes, five different board games, darts, cards, karaoke," said Alexis.

"We have junk food and healthy food, as well binge foods", giggle Naudia the oldest of the females.

"You know me" said Chalky, I am here if anyone needs me for anything," as he sat down grabbed the daily paper and propped his feet.

"Well, Jr.," said Derrick, the son right above Moreo Jr. "I guess we can shoot some ball or play my video gamer friends online," Jr. almost started salivating at the idea of playing "BlueOpp's" online with his new big brother and his cyber friends. He screeched out a yes, Derrick laughed a little he knew exactly how Jr. felt being so much age and distance between himself and his older brothers.

"Moreo," said Rena. "We sure are blessed to have such wonderful loving children. Look how well they get along after all this time and distance, it's like we haven't missed a breath."

Moreo grabbed Rena bear hug style, and kissed her smack on the lips lifting and twirling her around sweetly he said, " I believe there is a God that resides in us all that bonds us with His love, grace, and mercy. We are all His and we finally found one another."

How Rena loved this man God made for her. Her knight in shining armour. Her Moreo. She loved him more today than ever and she imagined it to grow out into the universe affecting the cosmos and causing others to love as she and her Moreo were.

Jr. was so wound up when they returned to the hotel, he kept begging " I want to go back to Derrick" and he had really good reasons why his parents should agree but this was his best. He said " Rena, Mariam is a girl who needs all the privacy she can get. If I'm not over there y'all can lock the door and you and dad will get some real privacy too finally."

"Sounds good big guy," said Rena. "But, we need you here with us for the park trip tomorrow morning. Plus no one lives there in that house, we all just met there today. Now get some sleep and rest up for tomorrow."

"Yes ma'am," said Jr. and was immediately off to sleep. She kissed his forehead and covered him up.

The week flew by and more and more friends were contacting the "Ellroys" Moreo's oldest best bud and classmate Tone was in town, he was rolling in the money with the new software applications he developed. "Moreo, my US Army hero, I want to throw you a welcome home gala and just in case I don't see you before you leave a remember you got a friend in me party."

Tone had rented a very nice glass front building with awnings and patio dining. Upon entering the smoky blue glass double doors, there was soft jazz music playing. Moreo wondered if he and Rena were dressed appropriately for this shindig. Rena was amazing in his eyes no matter what she had on. She sported a two-piece business casual dress suit, bluish grey with a flowing tail. He wore a charcoal grey business suit with an accompanying bluish grey tie, handkerchief and leather shoes to match his wife's lovely dress.

Everyone was here all of his and Rena's old classmates. The chatter was exciting and filled with joyous energy. Announcements of Moreo and Rena being the subjects of the party were made as well as free drink maximums. It was definitely a scene from " The Royals" and then it happened out of nowhere. It was as if the music stopped at once, the lights dimmed, and a spotlight shown directly on the entry way.

It was Denya, the one woman who has had power to cause Moreo to fail and lose all at her very whim. The moment of truth was here, and Rena began to prey for peace to have its way. She had on a long sultry black dress trimmed in blue shear ruffles that trailed and accented her cleavage as well as her long perfect legs and her black and blue heels were to die for.

Moreo saw Rena's insecurities show. For the first time he saw his morning glory shy away inside, the light in her eyes, he could see was challenged by the appearance of Mariam's mother. Moreo swallowed hard and quickly returned to Rena's side grabbing her hand, but Denya was reckless, careless, and without any remorse. She walked up to the coupled groped Moreo right in front of Rena. She slid that long leg that was uncovered and so seductively traced by the lace between Moreo's legs and slid her body up and down his rough enough for Rena to feel her intent.

"No, you devil," Moreo said as he pushed her off him by her face in his palm.

She came back at him dancing seductively. "You know you miss this, it's always here for you and I know you want it cause my body is aching for you."

"Moreo belongs to Rena," said Moreo. "Rena belongs to Moreo," he said as he led his wife out of the party. Back at the hotel he and Rena made love that night so good the only recording of that night will just stay in their memories.

It was their last day of socializing in the states before they had to board their flight back to Germany. This day was set aside for Moreo's mother Christine and her lifelong companion Marvin. Both were excellent cooks and were always eager to feed somebody. The house was warm and cozy and always felt safe. They ate and talked about everything under the sun. The food was good and plentiful and the ambience just right it was wonderful.

There was a knock at the door. Christine answered the door. She moved to allow the knocker entry. It was Denya, but she had someone with her.

"Oh, heck no!" said Marvin. "Denya what's going on in your head woman?" He continued.

"Moreo acts like he don't want this good, good no more cause that slave of his Rena is in the way. So, I brought her old owner back to remind her were her collar of loyalty truly lays, humph hahaha," she cackled. " Now let's see how you push him away like you did me Moreo."

Just then Chalky Sr. walked in Rena's heart stopped, not for desire, but for anger. She had never been so angry with one human being as she was right now with Denya.

She stormed past everyone heading towards the front door; when it happened. Denya had truly lost her ever loving mind. She touched Rena. She actually grabbed her sleeve like she was in authority over Rena.

"Why?" Rena without blinking had picked her helpless unknowing victim up and out the front door they went. Rena slammed Denya over the car and pummeled her about her face, neck, and body and kicked her a few times for Moreo, Mariam, Jr. and April (lowkey)

When Moreo felt that justice was served he stopped all of the commotion. They kissed everyone except Denya and Chalky sr. who never got a word in. Moreo and Rena thanked his parents for a lovely night and returned to the hotel, eagerly awaiting their flight back home.

"Wwirrrwurrrwiirrrropp, this is the police brrrnbrrm wirrrrr ma'am you are under arrest" said Moreo.

"Whatever for, officer?" Said Rena, in her sweet good girl voice, "for breaking all my rules and refusing to move that booty over so I can get some sleep." He pushed her over almost off the bed gripping her clothing so she wouldn't fall.

Rena squilled, " Moreo you better not drop me."

"Certainly not my lady," as he pulled her close to him and kissed her goodnight.

The story of Moreo and Rena

Dealing with death

It was the first day of spring 2023 and Moreo Ellroy's forty-seventh birthday and the year of his retirement from the Army.

Rena and Mariam who is now twenty-one attending the local University, were buzzing around making call backs to secure plans and tie up loose ends. This was going to be epic, the party that everyone who's anyone, on Post will want to be privy to, and it was open invitation.

Mariam made finger foods and punch, she also so brought chips and juice and pop. Rena whipped up a few dishes of some of her hubbies favorite southern homestyle foods to introduce to some of his colleagues who had never been to North Carolina or the United States for that matter. The party was catered by none other than "Food by Design".

The club house would seat at least two hundred at maximum capacity and Rena planned for that many hungry bellies and happy faces. Mariam and Jr. were stringing streamers and the "Happy birthday" banner. The hardwood floors had been freshly waxed and polished to a mirror shine. There was an amazing chandelier of crystal clear blue glass hanging in the very center of the hall. Every wall was a mirror.

The lights were dim adjustable and Rena new how to set the perfect scene with these. She smiled to herself at her shocking display when she appeared to Moreo at his birthday party tonight. "He's gonna go nuts" she thought to herself. " I can't wait to see his expression when he sees his real present walk in the room. Hehehe," she giggled aloud at the thought.

"His present, oh" Rena snapped back into her right train of thought. Was it old age or just a dreamy heart she always got forgetful when thinking of her Moreo. She had to remind the dealership that the car had to be placed exactly in the center front space behind the club house with the ribbon and bow facing the building.

Moreo was a Camaro fanatic, but he had not purchased a new car in years and Rena had just purchased the 2023 model. The dealer said it had the power of eight hundred horses and the body of an armoured tank. He said, "Little lady don't turn yourself into no missile" as he personally delivered it with a driver.

"Oh no it's for my husband, it's his birthday and his retirement gift from myself and the children."

"Lucky man" said both men simultaneously.

"Not luck at all," said Rena. "A good therefore blessed man. That's what he is. Luck had nothing to do with this. My husband is loved gentlemen, loved.

Mariam and Jr. were waiting in the main hall where the mirror room was. They looked disturbed.

"What is it?" Rena asked. Mariam handed her her own cell.

"I answered your phone Rena I'm so sorry. I saw "mommy" as your caller ID, so I thought I better answer."

"What is it Mariam?"

"Rena it's your mother. That was your brother calling from her phone. He said it was the only way he could find you since all of your children moved away."

"Mariam please," said Rena.

"Your mom passed last night in her sleep Rena," Mariam screeched out.

"Whoa whoa whoa hold up," said Jr.

"You don't tell nobody something like that, like that. Mariam, girl you ain't got no koof about yourself." He was an old soul alright. "Koof," he was a good old thirteen-year-old grandpa and he had a look on his face of disapproval of the delivery. He offered Rena condolences and a shoulder to cry on, but she refused his gestures. With a smile on her face she twirled around and continued setting up for the party.

Around six o'clock Moreo arrived blind folded and guided by Tony. There were so many people here Rena greeted everyone. All was going according to plan. Tony brought Moreo just on time as the guest expected. He parked where Rena designated so her man would not see his gift and she could spot him and go hide quickly.

Tony opened the door guiding Moreo through first, " Surprise!" the crowd roared as Tony removed the blind fold. Moreo was overwhelmed with all the faces that came to celebrate him. "I'm gonna cry" he thought, "Never" and he kept it moving greeting everyone and eyeing the room for his wife.

The children greeted him cheerfully, saying " happy birthday dad."

Then it happened, the lights went dim and the blue light above the chandelier shown down on the beautiful oriental area rug in the center of this seemingly marble polished hard wood floor. Long sultry legs trailed behind with an asymmetrical tail. At the bottom of those legs were ankles any woman would die for, upon feet sporting purple glassy looking seductive pumps. Above those legs, the knees and just a tidbit of thigh shown below fitted purple dress with a flowing tail trailing toward the back growing longer. Above the waste was a well-proportioned figure and bust line with a v-line overlap. "Deliciously classy" Moreo thought to himself as he gazed over his wife's attire and her locks were twisted and pulled up off her neck into a bun with a few left out for effect.

Moreo's mouth fell open Rena was absolutely breathtaking. A server handed him a glass of chardonnay as he approached his wife.

"Rena," he started, "You are absolutely breath taking my dear love." He kissed her and thanked her for setting this all up. Mariam and Jr. walked up smiling all goofy and giggly. They had never seen Rena look this good either, she was more than beautiful to them at this very moment, than she had ever been.

"She's fine dad, who dis said Jr. I won't tell Rena nothing if you let me get that number too!"

Both parents laughed. "Boy, you better back yo big head up off my wife," Moreo said with smirk and grabbed Rena and started dancing to their song, "Saved the Best for Last."

The party was very classy, and everyone enjoyed themselves. Mariam was proud that all of her finger foods were eaten. Although no cooking was involved, Rena taught her that even a sandwich made with love can taste like a steak. She loved her dad truly so, when her handmade foods disappeared, she saw it as her love for her dad made the mini sandwiches delicious. She just smiled and eagerly assisted the servers.

She thought "I can open a catering spot with Rena's help, it would be nothing hard." She told Jr. He just smiled and high fived her and said, "go for it!" They watched as their parents and the others danced and had a good time. Between the two of them they discussed their concern with Rena and her mom.

Jr. asked Mariam, " do you think she's a compartmentalist? I mean maybe she practiced displacement for so long that it's second nature. People who experience multiple traumas in life, develop this skill as a form of mental protection. Which can be later developed into being ingenious."

Mariam coughed and almost got choked on her words. " Jr. why do you know all of that, and how is it that I believe you, and I feel like you knew exactly what you were talking about? You're old dude, just like Rena says.

"Yeah, I know stuff because I like books, duh," he said as he rolled his eyes at Mariam and walked off to start helping to collect trash and clean up.

Moreo squealed like a schoolgirl when Rena escorted him out through the back door of the club house, which you had to walk through a huge stainless steel kitchen to get to. It was beautiful, jet black, shiny and sleek the driver tag said Mr. 300 and the License said BlacPantha with a picture of a panther custom made. Rena went all out. The leather seats were embossed with letters that spelled Ellroy. Moreo almost fainted he was truly beside himself. He kissed and hugged everyone at the party as if they all chipped in on it. He had Tony to take a picture of Rena handing him the keys and himself taking the bow off. The boy's back home would be happy for him finally choosing Rena, she gave him life and breath he never thought existed in this realm.

The party was coming to an end it was ten o'clock by now.

"Old people and children need to be in the bed by this hour" said Mariam. She looked at her little brother and said, "I guess I will drive your old self home with me," and he moved further away from her because he was trying to concentrate on his task and she was being silly procrastinating, and making jokes on folk so she didn't have to clean.

He knew her game. He's been around for thirteen long years and he was very serious about his business. Mariam shook her head and giggled at her dear sweet baby brother. "Old man," she thought and giggled a little to herself again. She adored Jr. and would move heaven and hell to protect that lil old dude.

Once back at the condo Mariam and Jr. excused themselves to prepare for bed and to give Rena and Moreo some private space.

Rena went on into the master bathroom. She was quiet as a mouse ever since they left the party. Moreo wasn't sure but he had a gut feeling it was bad. He walked into the restroom to find Rena undressed and balled up on the floor beside the tub filling with water, crying her heart out in silence.

"Oh no, what is my heart?" He approached her and kneeled by

his love. She grabbed his neck with both hands and plunged her head into his chest. Her sobs hurt him in the bottom of his belly. He just held her silently and rubbed her back, up and down as you would when trying to burp a baby. He waited patiently until she spoke.

"Moreo it's my mother, she passed last night."

Moreo was shocked to hear this news. "When did you find this out my dear," he asked.

"At the party just a few hours before you arrived. What am I going to do ,Moreo we have only been communicating openly for the past ten years, and five of which I have been here? I wonder if she knows I truly forgave her and loved her. We still had rough patches where I would cut off communication for weeks even months if things were heading in the wrong direction. I was only teaching her how she would be allowed to communicate with me and treat me as an individual.

"Moreo I really don't know this woman. I was getting to know her. I was learning her. Although I love her as a human being, I was learning to feel our family bond. I am a horrible daughter Moreo. Last month I cut her off because she started finger pointing at my dad again for why my life was how it was. It was both of them and I overcame it all. I just can't deal with all the dragging up old negative memories every time we talk. So I stop communication hoping she will get it. But, now it's too late to apologize. I am horrible." She sobbed.

Rena's husband helped her up and into the tub where he washed her back and hair while she sat in that tub crying. He kissed her every so often on her forehead. He didn't know what to do or say, he was just there. If he could do nothing else, he would be there for any questions or venting his love may have. He prayed hard and deep inside.

"Holy Spirit lead me, help me to soothe my wife. She is my good thing and she is hurt right now, and I feel helpless. Give me a word of encouragement or an act to do that will cause peace to abound." He finished washing Rena up and helped her out the tub, she was undone.

Rena was amazing, how did she hold that all in throughout this entire day and give him such a beautiful time? Love and devotion, that's how. He was very much devoted to her as well. He just was caught off guard. He had never had to console a wife before, who'd just lost a parent, he began to worry of his capabilities at this moment. He was a commander not a nurturer. "God, help me" he thought over and again.

Once in the bedroom Moreo caught a whiff of lavender, but none was burning. So he took that as angelic guidance. He went and got the wax burner and the lavender oil wax cubes and he put it on so the aroma would fill the air. He turned on some slow jazz music, very low and soft to the ears. Then he got the hot oil out and heated it up. He grabbed a couple of towels, and a half drank bottle of Chardonnay.

After patting his wife dry, (Rena didn't play that rubbing dry stuff, she had OCD about dead skin in towels and rubbing it back into your skin). That was another reason she hated shower curtains and would wash them so often a week-old shower curtain looked as if it had been around a while longer. "My babe will wash it holy" Moreo joked to himself. He thought it not a good time to joke openly with Rena.

He asked her to sit on the bed and he sat on her shrunk. He placed one towel across his lap covering his pants. He grabbed both of Rena's feet and placed them on the towel over his lap. He took the bottle of hot oil, poured some in his hands and rubbed them together and began, rubbing and massaging Rena's feet starting with her right foot. Moreo knew her feet were her weakness, and he felt the spirit of God come upon him and he began to speak.

"Rena, my love and dear sweetheart, you are the light of my day and God knew that you would heal and mend my broken emptiness. You did that babe and I am here now for you. Do you remember how horrible your mom was to you? She did not raise you God did. Not being funny but just being real, she tried to kill you and didn't fight to try to get you back. Now, I know this may hurt, but she was not your mother God was and is still. When my mother and father forsake me God will take me up, now babe God did that for you through the random different folk he used to assist you along your journey.

Now, she a human God used as a channel to get you here has passed. You are crying over a bond that never happened. You are doing this because you feel somehow still it was your fault she was horrible to you. You feel you were never in a right place with her, because she didn't love you properly. I know your heart Rena you're my rib. You must let it go. This woman that has past is not your responsibility. If she forgave herself and asked God for forgiveness and you, she will be fine. I will arrange for our flights as soon as you know the funeral arrangements."

"Moreo " said Rena, "you know me too well. I just wanted to feel the mother daughter connection that I never felt from her. I guess I'm being selfish because she died and we never established that. I never felt at home I always knocked on her door even when it was open. Unlike my siblings that she did raise, they just walked right in her front door. They felt welcomed and at home," something Rena never felt ever anywhere except now with Moreo and their family.

"Rena, I know you don't attend funerals for your own personal reasons, but this is one that I know you should attend to say your true final goodbyes. You will be fine I will definitely be by your side every step of the way."

He rubbed her feet so darn good she was relaxed and starting to doze off when she said, "I bless God for you my love. All that you have said is correct and I am well with what you have said. I love you Moreo Ellroy and I will forever honor and cherish you. You are a wise kind and loving and a necessary part of my of my existence." He covered his little beauty up and got in the shower and prepared himself for work the next morning.

The story of Moreo and Rena

Moving Back to the States (where and why?)

The year 2023 was flying by. It was already June and spring was warming to summer. Moreo had Tony, Van, Mariam, and Jr. on post. He had the Bishop of their parish sitting in the pool house with friends and neighbors of the Ellroys.

Moreo was a great planner. He insisted that Mariam needed to have all new clothing and school supplies for at least a year to take back to the states. He reassured Rena the savings would benefit them in the long run financially, especially with Jr. being in need of several uniforms. They never needed uniforms here.

They would be gone for at least three hours, Moreo could trust Mariam for that she was good at getting all she could out of what she had to spend. He gave her enough to look and talk and walk and shop for hours. So, Rena was out of the way at least two more hours and that would be perfect.

Van prepared Rena's favorites. The cake was a three tier German chocolate, topped with a bride and groom, that seem to resemble the couple very much. It was uncanny. She baked a lasagna and made tamales, cucumber sandwiches, and Moreo's buffalo wings, mac-n-cheese, fried fish, slaw, potato salad. It was definitely going to be some soul filled bellies today.

The seamstress delivered the gown and it was absolutely breath taking. Moreo squealed to think of how his bride was going to feel when she slipped her gown on for the first time. He had purchased and hidden a garter, girdle, white satin bra and panty set trimmed in shear blue lace. The dress itself had a floral design on which clear baby blue rhinestones shimmering across the breastplate and a split down the front that would gently reveal her left leg.

Jr. was dusting and taking all the trash out. He already vacuumed the entire four thousand square feet of their beautiful now already sold condo home. Jr. thought about how much he would miss this place the last five years have been the best of his thirteen on earth. He teared up and continued to tidy every nook and cranny. Two of the invited guests were also the couple who purchased their home. He wanted them to see it at its best as long as they were still living there. He was surely his father's son.

Tony was in charge of the grill and music. He also directed the truck driver when the matrimony aisle arrived. It was gorgeous, shaped like a heart or two people kissing. It was all white and the runner was a shimmering color blue and white green. It seemed to simulate water. Tony had the outside totally under control out back. The aisle was placed about twenty-five feet forward the last step exiting the door heading towards Rena's favorite side of the house. The ocean was everything to her and Moreo made sure to advise Tony of this. He had no doubts in Tony's ability to make all correct.

The seamstress also delivered Moreo's tuxedo. He decided to prepare himself for the event of his life. He and Rena were already married but, now he was going to give his baby her dream, a real wedding. He had been to the barbershop as soon as Mariam left out with Rena, so he needed to shower, brush his teeth and hair, lotion up for his baby and get dressed.

Mariam sent Moreo the text code that said he needed to be in place because they would be walking through the door in five minutes. He alerted everyone. Jr. went to the pool house to get everyone seated out on the beach side where they had white seats placed facing the aisle where they could see the bride exit the door of the condo. The bishop sat off on the side where there was a table and Van had a plate and drink for him waiting. He ate as the festivities arose to his part of the show.

"Why are we leaving the things in the car," Rena asked Mariam.

"Well," she paused. " I planned to get Jr. to help me bring it all in." Rena insisted on helping but Mariam just grabbed her hand and started singing and dancing encouraging Rena towards the door. She tapped on the door as if accidentally laughing and holding Rena's hand and lead on through the door right into Moreo standing dead front and center.

He was more gorgeous today than ever. It didn't take a rocket scientist to figure out what was going on here. She smelled the food outside, but now it's a heavenly aroma inside as well. There were ribbons and streamers everywhere white, and blue, and shear clear. Soft jazz music playing and Moreo.

"Oh Moreo" Rena said as she walked in closer to him. Mariam scooted on by to go find where she could be of help tightening up any loose ends.

Moreo approached Rena and grabbed her left hand. He knelt down before her and looked up into her eyes he said, " Marry me Juliette and I promise I will never leave you lonely. I will forever stand by your side, but you must be my bride."

"Well of course my love king, I'd marry you a thousand times over and over. You are stuck with me, buddy."

He removed the old wedding set he had previously given her and placed a brand new five carat diamond on her finger. "It's beautiful Moreo, almost as beautiful as you my lord," said Rena.

He escorted her into the room where her gown was laid out on the bed so elegantly. Her eyes lit up just as Moreo expected, she teared up and he did as well. His heart was very pleased when he made her happy. He lived to make his loved ones happy especially this woman right here.

"It's absolutely gorgeous Moreo, but you gotta send Mariam in here and you must go now, tradition, tradition," she giggled. Rena was happy. More happy than she had ever been as a living being, she had the best biological children the world could offer and her babies with Moreo were in the same bucket in her world.

Mariam entered the room just in time to assist Rena in zipping up the back of her beautiful gown. Rena was glowing as if she was a brand new twenty-one-year-old bride. Mariam believed Rena was absolutely ravishing in her gown. Rena sat on the edge of the vanity chair for Mariam to pin her locks up for the band of the vail to fit perfectly. She glossed her lips and lined her eyes. She put on some mascara to thicken her lashes but that was all she needed. Mariam stood back and smiled at the finished product.

"I'm sorry I can't help it, that's my mom as well," said a familiar voice. It was Alexis! She was here. "Oh mommy," gasped Alexis. "You're beautiful, queen. We are all here. I had to see you. Mariam has been so gracious in keeping the surprise and doing everything to keep you occupied. I just couldn't wait when this is your first official wedding. What can I assist with?"

Rena had Alexis to help stabilize her garter and help her with the glass slippers. Alexis also spread out the bouquet to look fuller and misted Rena with her favorite body spray. Rena was amazing. She was ready to join her groom.

As she walked to the back door heading toward the beach side, she saw Derrick waiting in his tuxedo on the left side. Awaiting to walk her down the aisle. The ladies dispersed and went to their respective places. Tony started the music it was perfect, Vanessa Williams' "Save the Best for Last." The temperature was absolutely amazing. Everyone was here, all of the children.

"Wow how did Moreo pull all this off right under my nose, he is completely wonderful." Rena thought. Derrick raised his right arm for his mother to grab. He had such a proud adoring looking on his face for his mother. They headed toward Moreo and Tony on left, while the two oldest daughter and Mariam were on right. The men had on all white tuxedos with baby blue cumberbuns and bowties. The women had on baby blue dresses with white trim around every edge and border. Rena took notice of the heart shaped aisle and she blushed, thinking of a picture Moreo took when he was first working his nerve up to propose. She loved it then, and now she was walking it.

Derrick respectfully nodded to Moreo as he handed his mother off to a man he was proud to call dad. Moreo took his brides hand the music stopped and they headed toward the Bishop, who had just risen from where he sat and stood before them with bible on podium and hands risen to call everyone to order and to stand for prayer. After the prayer for a blessed day and union he asked everyone to be seated and he began the wedding procedure. When he arrived to the vows a mic was handed to Moreo and these were his personal handwritten vows.

"Dear beautiful one, I searched the globe high and low for a place to trust my heart and rest my soul. I was a wanderer on a futile mission. I called to the moon and wished upon stars and yet there was no one for me. I finally had a talk with my father God and reminded him that he said," he pointed toward the sky, "man should not live alone. He took a rib and I wanted to know where did he place mine? Then I found you. Always there, we just never knew. My soul leaped the moment you said you loved me too. I wanted to blood bond you to me that very moment, but looking in your eyes I knew that I could trust you to be true to my heart, my mind, and my soul, your love nourishes me Rena baby right down to the marrow in my bones and I refuse to live life a day without you and I will never leave your side until my very last breath is gone." He placed her old band back on her finger as he had not given it back after removing it earlier.

This was so sudden Rena had not prepared any wedding vows, but she felt stirred in her belly enough to wing something. She asked Moreo if she may try, he handed her the mic. Rena was very nervous but she would give it her best. She wanted her lord king to truly understand what his being in her life truly meant to her and she spoke into the mic.

"Sometimes we are abused and battered throughout life. There are times when we feel so low, we just want to stop existing. We go on throughout life believing there is nothing left for us to do or contribute to. I was at my darkest hour in life my children were grown I had no work and I felt useless and as if darkness and loneliness would consume me in my voided place. Then God reminded you of me. He put me on your mind and awakened your soul to my secret cry out in the lonely darkness of my corner for you to come save me. You responded to my soul's cry and I have not shed one painful tear since. You have been my knight in shining armour and my friend, lover and confident. Every day for the rest of my life I shall be at peace for I trust in your guidance and dominion over me to keep me safe and secure for God has made you the one I question not and till my last breath is taken I will serve and love honor, respect, forsaking all others, in sickness and in health to you only shall I keep myself."

Jr. had the pillow with Moreo's wedding band he presented it to Rena. Her eyes twinkled at Moreo; he had thought of it all. She took the ring and placed it on his left ring finger and said, "With this ring I the wed."

The bishop went through all the formalities, but no one would object. So when he announced, "By the power of God invested in me I now pronounce you husband and wife. You may now kiss the bride," the crowed roared "yeah, congratulations, hoorah," and many other cheers filled salutations.

Moreo and Rena faced the crowd and the bishop made his last announcement. "I present to you ladies and gentlemen Mr. and Mrs. Moreo Ellroy." They walked out to greet their guest and prepare for the reception in the pool house. Rena had to go change her clothing and she chose an elegant black sleek dress that accented her shoulder and collar bone, which Moreo loved.

Days after the wedding the chatter of the move back to the states has the Ellroy house buzzing like a beehive. Everyone was excited about moving home and seeing relatives. The children talked about friends they had left behind five years ago. They were able to keep some of their relationships alive via the internet, face time and simple phone calls.

Moreo called his family to order on Sunday evening after church. He invited them to a meal at "Gold Carroll's" everyone truly were very eager to agree. Rena was always happy for Sunday evenings although she adored cooking and caring for her family, but these treats she looked forward to.

"Gold Carroll's was crowded with all of the Sunday regulars. They would be having to wait for an hour to be seated. That didn't bother the Ellroys as they always knew how to keep one another entertained during the wait.

Moreo started the most important discussion of the move back to the states. He wanted to know where everyone would feel was best for their family. He started his conversation with a clear stated path for the direction he wanted it to move toward. He said, " when we choose a home, we must consider several factors" and he listed all of the factors to consider and why it was important.

" I want to keep our family as close as we are, and I don't want outsiders having influence on our family dynamics."

1. Location must be central to two hours driving in any direction of our family and friends for the reason I previously stated.

2. Location must be by water and landscapes that assist Rena and her work.

3. The schools' systems must be top notch and truly educate children, because Jr. is still in school and we want his grades to stay up.

4. What ever the community is it must have low crime rate and low unemployment rate as well as a low poverty rate, because of what I would like to keep my family safe from.

5. My last reason for the discussion is the location we decide upon must be a place known for warm weather. Rena and I are getting older and age thins skin and blood, this point I bring for reasons of the elders I know of who have told me of how painful it is being cold old and having arthritis."

Rena laughed out cause not only did she not have a thyroid but, she also had arthritis. "Moreo, my always thinking hero, saving me years ahead of time. That's truly why I am loving you for so long" Moreo pumped his chest out as if he knew he had it all under control. He was the man for his family, and they all let him know they knew it.

After they had dinner and returned home, they all had their baths and hung out in the living area for a while chatting of all the possible places they could be moving to. Florida came up Daytona and Orlando were mentioned by the children. They thought of an absolute perfect place for their mom Rena. Moreo had passed them a sweet spirit of love, kindness, and concern for others.

"Oh Moreo," said Rena after she knew the children were fast asleep.

"Yes Rena," he said.

"Come here lover boy," then she purred purrrrrrrdrrrrah " can we cha cha my darling?"

Moreo smiled his half curled lip smile an tilted an invisible cowboy hat at the little miss, and said, "Ma'am I reckon I'd be honored twirl a heel or two," Rena giggled because she could imagine the cowboy suit as Moreo hankered toward her as if his gun belt and boots were much to heavy for him, causing him to appear bowlegged and she giggled out of control.

Moreo started the dancing and low and behold for the very first time ever Moreo won. Rena was off her game. She was being too silly. It may be the fact they were moving back home soon, or it could be the fact that she secretly always wanted to know what would Moreo expect from a love slave before she got to old to perform his requirements. She giggled at the thought.

Moreo yelled, " I win, and you now belong to me, sexy bunny."

"Sexy bunny, Moreo, so you want a bunny huh?"

He said, " Yeah just hop around from one side of the room to the other."

"Hahaha that's not sexy Moreo," she said.

He said "I am going to hunt some rabbit and I hear there's a sexy bunny out here in these here woods."

Rena hopped to hide behind the curtain, he cornered her, she hopped toward the master bathroom and he blocked her. She hopped toward the closet door and he slammed the door to block her.

"Hey pretty, pretty bunny," Moreo said as a demented Elmer Fudd. "I'm a hunting bunnies," Rena squealed as Moreo grabbed her and tossed her on their bed gently. "I think I caught me self a bunny rabbit brahahaha." Rena shut off the lights by clapping twice and the Ellroys bonded sweetly before falling fast asleep.

Moreo and Tony had left to go house hunting in the states. They planned for a month. This was so they had time to truly seek around the areas the family seemed to truly agree on. Warm beach weather and secluded from massive amounts of chaos. Time was of the essence. Moreo was already discharged their home was sold and the only thing they were waiting on was the home they would be moving to. This was huge and Moreo took Tony with him not only to give him a vacation, but because he trusted Tony's opinion and wisdom in these matters. Tony had struck a place of honor in Moreo's heart and not many men had that effect on him.

They found the perfect home. Rena would go nuts Moreo thought. He told Tony, "This house with the wrap around porch log cabin style framework and the huge bay window facing the lake is going to run my wife nuts. She won't have a beach, but her own private access to this lake will be perfect for her."

The town was perfect. Castlewood was right in center of Myrtle beach South Carolina and the Savannah beach in Georgia. No, they were not directly on the beach but no more than 20 miles away. The schools were 4A and that was just good enough for Moreo's concern for Jr. There was a crime rate of one percent and poverty and unemployment was not one of Castlewood amenities. Thank God, Moreo had found a secure place for he and his family members to call their new home.

Tony knew some people that knew some people and the closing went divinely orchestrated. Things went smooth and by the end of the time allotted for this trip their task was very much completed.

They both were truly ready to return to their families. Moreo and Tony agreed they would forever be in one another's life. They found that they empower one another and friendships such as theirs only came once in a lifetime. They were mature enough to know they were too old to find another brotherly soul to connect with in this lifetime, therefore they would keep each other contact information.

Back in Wolfsburg, Moreo showed his family pictures of the landscape, inside the home, and he talked about everything under the sun from the weather in Castlewood to the friendliness he observed in the people. He noted how clean and well kept the roads were and clean and fresh the air is.

His family was excited and ready to move. They truly loved and trusted him, he never failed them, and they had no doubt dad had found a secure, safe, lovely new home for them. This made life easy for Moreo to navigate, his tribe had all faith in him and supported his goals and decisions. He knew he was a man a real man after God's own heart. He was not sad about retiring. He didn't feel a loss. He felt loved and empowered. Plus, he was ready to travel and assist Rena on some of her ventures and life was their oyster and he could finally sit back and enjoy chewing the bite he took.

The True Journey Begins

The Ministry of Moreo and Rena's Existence

All these episodes in life prior to moving back to the United States were directly ordered by the Most High Creator God. His Devine guidance lead Moreo and Rena back to one another. After the necessary lessons they would need to stay strong in the spiritual principles it would take to take their divine life missions to the next level. God needed them strong enough within themselves first with HIM alone as their only director. Then He trust them to stay on course even in their love affair with each other here on earth that they stay their course. They both were notorious for allowing relationships and bad circumstances stemming from bad situations in those relationships to derail them. Rena was side tract from being a functioning member of society. Moreo was affected in his work performance and retaining crewman as well as his teams respect. For lack of a better word his subordinates thought him to be weak when it came to women and consumed in finding more heart break woman after woman.

Once they were settled down in life home now being in Castlewood it had become very much realized that Moreo and Rena would be traveling and life coaching married couples all over the country. Mariam decided on Florida A& M University as the college she would attend, and Jr. chose to finish high school with his mom Rena homeschooling him. That worked well for everyone. Rena was an excellent teacher and very patient. She studied her students every movement during quiet reading or work study times.

Rena could tell by after a few weeks of observing her student every time they were stunted with a question or word or just simple comprehension of a statement or term. It was because she was a single mom for so many years and although she had no parenting tools to start with she was observant very analytical and she had strong empathy toward her fellow man so it was without fail truly easy for her to find a weakness in her fellow human. Her vow to God was to assist and build everyone she could up from their own weakness through His love and divine guidance and she did so always. This made her a very good teacher and all of Jr.'s state exams proved him to excel above those who attended the well to do private schools.

Rena was gifted to be a watcher from birth so no matter what she was experiencing she was also taking in every observance, aspect, and lesson of the time, occurrence, or occasion of life. Even when she was very young her beloved dear belated grand mother would say, " Rena, you are well past your years in wisdom. There are many flakey women out here in their thirties and forties that don't quite have your common sense."

She was only eight the first time she could remember her grand mother telling her this, and about the cull at her birth and explaining to her that when she sees things they are not ghosts. They are lost or trapped souls. She said they would not hurt Rena but that they could cause Rena to harm herself by abruptly trying to flee. She taught Rena how to harness all of her gifts and to channel them. Yet, it took Rena having her twins and three battles with cancer and the loss of her beloved grand mother and favorite cousin Valerie, for her to wake up and look alive. Once she owned the value of her turmoils in life and the unobtainable wisdom she harnessed from being the one to mine her caves. She now was a well of love to which humanity would benefit from, on a level that her Grandmother's lessons would impact creation itself. Rena took on the Entire Armor of God and welcomed the charge it seemed the world was calling Moreo and herself to keep with them.

People wanted this thing they had. People wanted love. They wanted God and acceptance from each other. People were suffering in silence in marriages that lacked stimulation, romance and passion. There were many marriages suffering from financial issues whether it be because the man was the sole provider to either the woman being lazy or she making more money. There was a common theme where the women were the sole provider and the men were being lazy.

The couple traveled and toured the country usually free of charge and all accommodations were provided including travel and dining in addition to the lodging and whatever amenities that were attached to it. They were a highly sought-after power couple. They were walking bibles. The two of them were exactly what the word means when it said double edge sword. They both were nothing but the truth. Moreo was more the cut that took out that old rotten stagnant thinking, he was and fire ball, and Rena was the cut that took you to the healing phase removing the last layer of film left from contact with whatever caused the issue in the first place. She was the cushioning. They both were strategic during the phase that they coined "Speed Therapy" it's set up was two tables and four chairs.

During "Speed Therapy" a couple comes up but they can not be husband and wife, to eliminate any sorts of conflict and confusion, although every attendant was a married couple not during this part. This is a part where the women get to ask Moreo a serious personal question regarding their husband and get honest uncut feed back. Likewise, the men get to sit across from Rena and do the same. As you can understand "Speed Therapy" requires disclosures and privacy statements all over it. So, indeed it cannot be handled recklessly. This was Rena and Moreo's life's work.

San Diego was a beautiful thriving city of lights, life, and partying, but love was absent, and the city was vacant and void of earth and harmony therewith. It was a cement, tar, smog mess and the people were good looking attractive yet, hollow, shallow, and clone like. They were without the spirit of love. They were only acting out emotions that were expected within being a human. But none knew the truth of love. This is why they were incapable of protecting their lovers from pain and heart break. They didn't understand their responsibility and role in how another person is treated and triggered to behave or react.

Many of the questions at this "KaPal Wow" as they coined this part of the sessions and yes, Moreo named it, was pertaining to ex's and disrespect toward the new mate. A lot of the women were showing signs of severe frustration and turning up their noses. Some of them shifted uncomfortably in their seats, because they were either experiencing at this moment or already have and they believed it was mishandled by them being Christian.

During one of the early morning sessions a question came from one of the attendees of the crowd on this topic on ex's being disrespectful and ratchet. The question was, " how do you stay holy during a period where your spouse's ex keeps trying to seduce your mate. You know without a doubt your mate loves you and only you, but this person is so determined to destroy what you have by any means necessary."

The petitioner remained standing in the crowed so the answer may be directed back to them. She was a very petite fair skinned blonde haired lady, dressed in a blazer and pleated dress. She wore red framed glasses that matched the red dress she sported. She was young and very well spoken. Yet her question seemed that it would not become someone with her demeanor. She looked very mom like, school teacher, Sunday school-ish, you know the type no one would think to cause any harm to. Lies! When it comes to matters of the heart believer and nonbeliever alike, we are in Satan's realm while we walk this here earth realm. That means all is fair in love and war. If you want your love to last sometimes you gotta do battle against spiritual principles and sometimes it may lead to a physical activity.

With this question arising Moreo smiled his little witty smirking smiles and handed the microphone over to Rena. The crowd suddenly erupted in hearty laughter as Moreo had previously spoken of an incident Rena had with his ex, when someone asked, " what do you supposed to do when your spouse is in a physical altercation?"

Rena giggled as she took the mic. She stood very close to the podium as she held tight to one of its sides. She was nervous fore; she knew she would need the full-on presence of the Holy Spirit to guide her answering such a touchy question. She asked for a quick pause to gather herself. The crowd sat patiently in wait for her to proceed. They wanted to hear the response as many of them were dealing with such matters currently.

She prayed softly but distinctively into the mic. "Dear sweet precious holy loving spirit of the living God arrest and direct my tongue with truth, wisdom, and sound righteous insights on the issue at hand. Let me only speak what is correct and just only." She raised her head and scanned the crowd looking to connect with her audience. She said "Amen," and began her speech.

Well, we all know that there are times that seem to arise were altercations appear unavoidable yet, in most situations God's Spirit inside you, let me interject and state, you must nourish the spirit portioned to dwell inside you. Just like your physical body needs foods. Your spiritual body needs to eat as well. I use the bible, and many other spiritual texts to keep myself on the moral path of "The Way." I walk out in nature to connect with the great mother clay of creation, because in my natural state nature and I are one and she nourishes me while I evolve into the being God created me to be she said in a drifting wonder. A smile that took you off with her to wherever sweet place she went briefly. "So, for example," she said getting back on task.

"I, being delivered from a violent temper and random outbursts in my lashing out on the world, had my salvation and delivery many years before Moreo and myself united. So imagine how I felt when I was placed in an awkward position one night in the states years back when Moreo and I were being celebrated. My husband's ex sexually assaulted him while I was on his arm. This infuriated me, but we were being celebrated by all of our classmates and Moreo was the man of the hour. This party was classy, and all eyes were on us. This heffa was trying it hard. I was humiliated and embarrassed, enraged wasn't the word. Inside my head I made excuses to pummel her, just when I mentally cried out "Father help me" I felt myself squeeze my loves hand almost instinctively as he is my protector on earth, he was already responding more than I actually expected. Trust me it was God's Spirit it happened simultaneously on a level of being on one accord. I took that as my sign from God that Moreo and I were truly linked spiritually, and he felt my anguish and removed my anxiety before it could have its full way with me. I love that man."

She looked toward Moreo and blew him a heartfelt loving kiss. He caught it and place it over his heart. Rena continued. "Moreo had just defended his love with her against the woman who had in times past had power cause him to lose it all. This woman is the reason he has been crushed and brought down to his knees. There was a calmness that took over my spirit at that very moment. I knew I trusted Moreo to honor and keep vows. I knew my man loves God and me, so, patience worked her perfected peace that time.

"No not every time will you be able to get away incident free. As my husband spoke to you earlier about, what to do when your spouse gets into a physical altercation. My husband explained to you that no one is anyone's punching bag or door mat. What you cannot avoid do not beat yourself up. You thank God you made it out alive and free you repent and keep moving. That is an incident not a lifestyle. Don't hold yourself prisoner to short comings you will never get to enjoy the fullness in the beauty of true salvation." She ended her talk by blowing a kiss to the petitioner and to the rest of the audience and took her seat beside her love.

The next city on the map was Brooklyn, New York and the unavoidable theme of this crew was finances and who wore the pants in the family. There was an undertone in the room as if whoever made the money was supreme ruler. This was a total mishap and an unfortunate belief system that has been the demise of fifty percent of marriages. Yes, finances were the number one enemy here. Moreo and Rena were about their father's business, when one question came up that stopped them both in their tracts with a deja vu effect.

They heard her correct alright and they knew full well what she said but Moreo insisted she repeat her question. She was a frumpy short homely looking lady. She was dark-skinned sporting an afro that appears to be trimmed and well kept. She wore a black and white blazer and dress pants. She did not look feisty at all but, when she asked her question it was loaded with a gargantuan of emotions.

Her question was, "Why should I stay in a marriage with a man who promised me the world. I left family and everything I knew to be my safety and security to be with him. Then he loses everything to his ex and their children because she had a loss of affection case on him that had not been closed on when we got married. I feel like I was misled and trapped in poverty. Why should I stay? It's not my fault he was whorish so why should I pay?"

Moreo and Rena both felt compelled to speak on this and Moreo went first. He started out with, "My first problem with the question at hand is where is the love and caring nurture that causes a woman to stand with her man anyway?"

Rena interjected, "God's word says that you become one flesh two are now twined into one." Therefore, it's both parties' finances, not just the one who is in the actual labor force."

"You are a team." Moreo stated, " and when one falls short the other should step up." I was and still is an Alpha male yet, my wife had to bail us out of a situation that my past discrepancies caused. We went from a quarter million in the bank down to rubble. I and my mental man psyche was crushed inside. It was hell to see how my past was having a negative effect on my marriage and it was sickening to my soul. I felt empty inside and less than a man.

Rena spoke. "My husband is a true provider and protector of his family and he was losing himself daily. I knew he would not agree, so I went behind his back and got work. I saved every penny as he could not get wind of my having money. It would only have him more concerned and insecure. Although my being sneaky was nerve wrecking and he was starting to question his ability to sexually satisfy me. My main concern was to alleviate my husband's stress and bring his mind some comfort. No, my plan was not to put on any pants nor to enter the workforce totally. I only wanted our family in a position of upward movement and my husband's mind to be at ease."

Moreo interjected. "My wife did what she had to do to save me mentally and emotionally. Yes, at first I was distraught, but, when it was done and over, I understood truly what help meet meant. I just hate I was so hard hearted to the fact. As a woman asking this question, or a man for that matter, I ask you, where is your loyalty, and where does your heart lay? "For better or worse" is nine times out of ten directly related to financial issues. When we say these vows, we say them not with an image of the worse. We tend to falsely imagine our marriage will be without fault or errors. This is a fairytale blatant lie deliberately concocted by the enemy of our souls himself. He does not want marriage between a man and his wife to be harmonious. Therefore, he and the media paint a false picture of perfect marriages and what they are supposed to look like. Now we reach for that goal and when our lives don't look like the falsity, we tend to find failure in what is not failing."

Rena spoke but she had a question for the lady as well as any other member of the audience who would be willing to answer. " When you were lonely, feeling like you would never find or be loved, did you give God all the stipulations you required for you to be stable with your love? Did you tell God give me a person who will always have money and no problems? No, I will answer that. You know why I know the answer is No? Because the God I serve would have left you alone and lonely. He would have never sent you one of his children. You see, God loves all of His children and would never want them mistreated or misused financially nor in any other form. Any man that wants to be a sole provider will be crushed internally by such a loss due to their own past behaviors. Love will make you see this pain and run to his aid not turn your back." Moreo and Rena both said into the mic at the same time, " Children of God who are married couples are the Power Couple to be!"

They went from city to city tackling some of the most important discussions in the Christian marriage world. The Ellroys seem to be God's very own magic wand for healing many marriages and leading folk with godly sound wisdom. There was very much cha cha dancing in between. They were good at keeping their love life spicy and alive! Rena was very good at knowing when he was spent, and she would intervene and when she was burnt out or having writers block, he would intervene and bring her peace and solace. They shared this everywhere they went with all who would receive their message.

One last trip I'd like to share with you is when they were in Las

Vegas, Nevada. These folk had more issues between their children getting alone with one another and or the stepparent. These were very serious issues in marriages that blend ready made families and it placed mostly the females in a bad situation. Mostly because daddies' girls don't like sharing their dad's with new females who are not their mom. There are also issues with step siblings who don't want to share their parent with children who are not their parents. So this subject was a matter of their hearts to the core. They both were concerned with the spirit of love ruling and abiding within head of the houses.

Moreo spoke first. "When I sought God for myself and in righteousness on the matter of my children and bringing a new mom into their lives. My wife has older children, so my children did not have to share me as a hands-on father figure with them. Yet, my wife was still mother to her children long distance. She was also observant loving and kind to my children. Within months you could not tell she was not their mother biologically. The issue we faced was my own insecurities which rubbed off on my children's psyche as well. My daughter said things that I didn't approve of but, my wife is a God-fearing woman. She heard the pain instead of the words. I suggest that we all take a look at our salvation and our connection to God through his precious holy loving spirit. Because without him you will be fighting a losing uphill battle. This world today caters to wrong being what rules and right being what is shunned. That's why God created Rena and me, for such a time as this."

"There is a way that seems right to a man in his own eyes, but in the end is penury (destruction)," Rena started. "I gave birth to my children and my bond to them comes without question. Yet, when I am open and able to love a man, I must also love that which came from him as well. If I love him then all that he is and comes with is what my concern is. We look at children in such a way that we don't distinguished their brains as developing at all times and receiving and processing information correct but also warped as well. It is the warped thinking that we must be alert and ready to attack as soon as the devil rears his little head in the minds of our children. They are still developing their system of beliefs and insecurities are rampart when merging to different families coming from total opposite backgrounds. We can not allow our children to destroy our home. Even when it comes to bringing chaos to the house it is " Forsaking all Others." When you put your foot down to your children that there will be harmony in your home even if it means removing them to acquire that peace. Usually they will see a united fort and back down to align themselves to the program or they may actually desire to leave. Parents can not take this personal. Don't allow others including your children to take your home out. One day they will have their own family and quite possibly be extremely happy. If you allowed them as a child to destroy your marriage now, you're dealing with bitterness and resentment. You are the captain of your own seas your spouse and yourself. Your children are in the home temporarily and they will get alone for the purpose of having a safe place to learn and grow in. Children must sometimes be reminded. That a parent's home is a springboard and not their final destination. Parents you must want to protect your marriages. You can not put anything before it. God will give you all the words and direction you need if in fact you yield to His Sovereign Rule. There is nothing" -at this point Moreo joined her in finishing the statement- "my God can't handle."

Moreo and Rena went on to travel as beacons of hope nationally and eventually globally. They tackled real life issues plaguing the marriages in the body of Christ town by town city by city until they were well up into their sixties, when Moreo started to lose his power to rise to the occasion of the cha cha dancing.

He was now sixty-eight and had not experienced the loss of this strength until now. Rena looked even more sexy to him now after all these years. She was fully grey headed and proud of it. She had gained a little around the bottom. To him his baby was aging just right. He struggled with not being able to perform.

He sought help from the medical world. He tried creams and gels you name it he tried it. Alas there was nothing left for him to try besides prayer, which is always in order, he tried psychotherapy.

Rena joined Moreo in his quest for there was nothing he could face without her beside him to cheer and support him on. Although it wasn't bothering her as it would seem to bother him.

One day after therapy Moreo asked Rena to take a sit by the lake behind there home. "Rena, I know I'm an old man now and I can never get my youth back. I wasted so much of my younger years with the wrong women that once I realized it was you my soul sought all along, well time had gotten the best of us both.

I forgive and kick myself sometimes simultaneously for that. But, that's neither here nor there. I know how you enjoy when we make love it gives you life and energy and vitality. It seems to perk you up and wake up your creative juices and imagination along with the nature scenes and the Holy Spirit. Now, my body is giving way to age and my youth has dwindled, how can I keep my butterfly fluttering? I am alive when you're happy and enjoying life fully. Now, I deprive you of one of your joys in life. How will we go forward? Do you need sex and how often? Will I be pushed aside for a toy? Will you grow bored with me? There are so very many questions in my head running me mad. I could not concentrate on chopping the wood up for the fireplace, and I know you will get me for that if your little feet get cool. You must know there is nothing in forever that I would not do for you my love. I will take pills drinks exercise whatever, just stand by me while I deal with this Rena. Baby I swear to you my undying love and if you continue on with me Rena it would truly make me the happiest man to exist in my time."

Rena spoke very slowly, calmly, and steadily as she looked at her sweet lover all five feet four inches pushing it. His chocolate brown eyes, and his head barely grey his caramel colored skin doesn't look a day over forty and his beautiful lips always teaching kissing and soothing her soul. She kissed his lips gently and said.

"Moreo, you came, you came when all my hope for living had failed me. You came when you wanted to do something different. You came because God caused me to be a priority in your heart. You came and my life has only been more enriched by the life of you. We are bigger than sex. We came to earth for God's purpose and once we realized that he brought us together in his perfected timing, we have done nothing but blossom. As far as your libido and how are you going to keep me. Moreo where am I going at sixty-nine years old.

Now we have not been together thirty or forty years but what we have some folk couldn't accomplish had they been born and died together.

"You are my buddy, you are my pal. You are my confidant and the hero of my now. I will never need sex as much as I need to hear you breathe my love. You see for as long as I'm alive I need you alive and alright. My concern is our health and riding these later years out together gracefully.

"You see my love we are more and have always been more than sex although we did do it right hehehe," she giggled at her own statement. " We are companions we are lovers, we are sister and brother, mother and father, but above all Moreo Oliver Ellroy we being children of the Most High Creator God, are best friends. You hear that babe? 'A man who has friends must first show himself friendly, but there is a friend that sticketh closer than a brother.' Besides Jesus Moreo, I am your friend."

Moreo and Rena lived well into their late eighties early nineties spreading the gospel of God's love affair with mankind through connection with one another one person at a time. They explained to everyone that twin flames mean two original fires God ordained from the beginning to complete a mission that he designed them alone to do as a unique couple amongst the many. They used their light to guide you on parts of your journey. Now, who did your life experiences prepare you to help?"